For Otto Ubermaier,

This isn't

Rumpole, but maybe

you'll like it anyway.

Regards,

Dan Komstein

Something Else

MORE SHAKESPEARE AND THE LAW

DANIEL J. KORNSTEIN

authorHOUSE®

AuthorHouse™
1663 Liberty Drive
Bloomington, IN 47403
www.authorhouse.com
Phone: 1-800-839-8640

Published by AuthorHouse 1/5/2012

ISBN: 978-1-4634-4623-9 (e)
ISBN: 978-1-4634-4624-6 (dj)
ISBN: 978-1-4634-4625-3 (sc)

Library of Congress Control Number: 2011914208

FOR MY GRANDSON

CHASE SUMNER RIDDER

Tarry a little. There is something else. . . .
The law hath yet another hold on you.

The Merchant of Venice, 4.1.302, 344.

TABLE OF CONTENTS

PREFACE

We are never done with Shakespeare. He is so large and deep, so subtle and profound, so full of insight and understanding, that we keep making new discoveries and having new thoughts about him and his plays. Shakespeare burrows into our conscious and subconscious, rattling around in there for a while, until some new connection is made, until a new nerve synapse is created, and we have an idea that had not come to us before. Just when we think we have said all we have to say about Shakespeare, we get another thought and find something else to say. I learned that lesson for myself, and it led to this book.

This volume is a sequel of sorts to a book of mine published by Princeton University Press in 1994 about Shakespeare and the law. For the title of that earlier book, I drew on the most famous line in *Henry VI Part 2*, and, adding a crucial question mark, called it *Kill All the Lawyers?* and subtitled it *Shakespeare's Legal Appeal*. In that book I discussed a number of Shakespeare's plays and explored how they might be interpreted under our contemporary American law. I thought I had put into *Kill All the Lawyers?* all of my ideas on the subject. I thought I had exhausted the topic. I was wrong.

I had more, I had something else, to say. As the years passed since 1994, I found other issues that intrigued me about Shakespeare and the law. I could not let go of the topic, not completely. It kept on fermenting in my mind. My day job as a full-time practicing lawyer continued to bring home to me the relevance of Shakespeare's plays to my profession. And watching the plays from time to time vividly demonstrated to me the legal significance of a line or a scene. In short, I was not yet done with Shakespeare and the law.

This little book is the result. It is the "something else" I had to say; hence the title. It is a grab-bag of comments on various legal aspects of the Bard's plays. What ties them together, however, what unifies them, is the theme of Shakespeare and the law.

Exploring Shakespeare and the law is extremely useful and beneficial. "I am struck," writes NYU law professor Kenji Yoshino in his excellent 2011 book *A Thousand Times More Fair: What Shakespeare's Plays Teach Us About Justice*, "by how many contemporary issues of justice Shakespeare does illuminate." I completely agree. I also agree with Professor Yoshino that Shakespeare's "work stimulates conversation about justice that might not otherwise be possible." That is why I had to write the book you are holding in your hands.

The first chapter considers, from the point of view of legal proof, what Mark Twain has to say about who wrote Shakespeare's plays. The next two chapters consist of moot court briefs based on *Hamlet* and *The Merchant of Venice*. Then comes an essay on *Coriolanus* as a study in democratic theory. After that follow chapters on *The Comedy of Errors*; the unethical judges in Shakespeare's plays; Shakespeare's views, as glimpsed in *Henry V*, on the law of war; and Richard III and the mystery of the princes in the Tower. The final chapter is an imaginary encounter between Shakespeare and a modern literary agent descended from Christopher Marlowe.

As Portia tells Shylock, I now say to you: "Tarry a little. There is something else. . . . The law hath yet another hold on you."

Some portions of this book originally appeared in somewhat different form in the *Tennessee Law Review* (chapter 1) and the *New York Law Journal* (chapters 2 [briefs for Hamlet], 3 [briefs for Shylock], 4-7 and 9).

CHAPTER I

The Never-Ending Riverboat Debate
(Or Mark Twain on the Shakespeare Authorship Question)

Shakespeare stands on a pedestal high above world literature. He bestrides English literature like a colossus. So exalted is his status that it makes him a prime target, an easy mark, for contrarians or those seeking to make their own reputation by challenging the champion. As a result, some people want to knock Shakespeare off his lofty perch, and so they ask barbed questions.

One such question is: Who wrote Shakespeare? It is an old question, centuries old in fact, a vexing, perplexing, and nagging question, and one that never dies.

Probing further, interested people want to know: Was the unschooled country bumpkin from Stratford the true author of all those wonderful plays, sonnets, and poems filled with scholarly references, intimate knowledge of human nature, and far-reaching experience of the world? Or was it someone else, whose education, professional training, and life experience were a more probable and fertile soil for such literary works to grow in? These intriguing inquiries form the core of the Shakespeare authorship debate.

The authorship debate continues unabated and with great energy even to this day. Almost four hundred years after Shakespeare's death in 1616, we still wonder and argue over the authorship question. The public controversy over the 2011 film "Anonymous" illustrates the point. The premise of that film is that the plays and poems traditionally attributed to William Shakespeare are actually the work of Edward de Vere, seventeenth Earl of Oxford. Reaction to the movie was swift. Almost

1

immediately, the film's premise was vigorously challenged. "A hoary form of literary birtherism," "fiction that wants to confuse itself with fact," were just two of the more colorful criticisms published in the New York Times. The one I liked best called the movie "a vulgar prank on the English literary tradition, a travesty of British history and a brutal insult to the human imagination."

But despite such dismissive comments, the controversy is very much alive. Experts still write erudite books on the subject, the most notable of recent ones being James Shapiro's excellent book *Contested Will: Who Wrote Shakespeare?* and Stephen Greenblatt's *Will in the World.* Even learned justices of the U.S. Supreme Court take sides, publishing their extracurricular opinions in law review articles, speeches, and moot courts. Although I am an unrepentant, unreconstructed Stratfordian, some people whose judgment I respect favor the Oxfordian thesis. In short, many of us do not seem to tire of the arguments pro and con, even if — or precisely because — there is no definitive, universally accepted, answer. The quest itself fascinates.

Such a long-running, inconclusive debate might benefit from a creative, innovative approach. Suppose we let our minds relax a little bit and try to come up with a different entry point into the authorship controversy. Suppose we search for a happy metaphor. After all, a powerful metaphor can excite the imagination; a vivid new image can leave an indelible imprint on the mind. It stays there and supplies a fresh way of thinking about a stale subject.

We have at hand just such a happy, powerful image for the Shakespeare authorship debate. And we can thank the celebrated author of *Tom Sawyer* and *Huckleberry Finn* for it. It is a charming and stimulating image drawn from life on the Mississippi River that Mark Twain wrote so much about. It is an image that contemplates a giant of American literature commenting on the giant of English literature.

A NEW METAPHOR

Imagine a twist on the famous episode of Huck Finn and his friend the runaway slave Jim rafting down the Mississippi. Conjure instead a small boat moving forever along what Twain called a "monstrous big river," so big it seems to have neither beginning nor end. Call it, because it is everlasting, the River of Time. The boat has only two people on it, ordinary people without much formal education (like Huck and Jim), but (unlike Huck and Jim) each with a deep, abiding, amateur's love of Shakespeare. As the boat floats on the great River of Time, the two riders take turns reading Shakespeare's plays aloud to each other. And they endlessly talk and vigorously argue about who wrote those plays.

This never-ending riverboat debate is a good, memorable, Mark Twain-inspired image for considering the controversy over who wrote Shakespeare. The source of this helpful metaphor is worth investigating.

The Mississippi River was where, one hundred and fifty years ago, a young Mark Twain had wonderful adventures and piloted steamboats. Up and down that mighty river, Twain tells us, he "discussed, and discussed, and discussed, and disputed and disputed and disputed" the Shakespeare authorship question. For the next fifty years, up until his death, the creator of Huckleberry Finn and Tom Sawyer was interested in the Shakespeare authorship debate. Twain took a controversial stand in that debate, drawing on Shakespeare's legal references to conclude that the author was not the uneducated, contemporaneously uncelebrated Man from Stratford, but instead a prominent, practicing London lawyer with a literary bent, probably Francis Bacon.

Yet Twain's contribution to the debate has been neglected for far too long. His contribution is important despite the doubt he unintentionally cast on his own conclusion about Shakespeare's identity. In fact, Twain's doubt should become an instructive part of the debate. In short, trying to solve the evidentiary puzzle of who wrote Shakespeare requires at least a nodding acquaintance with Mark Twain's testimony, and Twain's evidence deserves to be carefully weighed in the balance.

REVERSING THE PREMISE OF INTELLECTUAL BIOGRAPHY

The premise of intellectual biography is that the life illuminates the work, but this premise is not universally accepted. It is itself actually rather controversial. One school of literary thought, which lists Flaubert, Proust, and the New Critics among its members, thinks that biography is irrelevant when interpreting the literary work. Instead, they say, the work yields its meaning only through close reading. According to this school, only the author's work counts, not the author. The author must make posterity believe that he or she never existed.

A competing school disagrees and finds it difficult to separate the work from the life. After all, a writer writes out of his or her whole life experience, and the world wants to know how poems, stories, paintings, music, and great plays come into being. Sainte-Beuve, the nineteenth-century French critic, famously used a biographical method that disassociated the author from his or her work. If the large number and great length of today's literary biographies are any guide, readers want to link books to their authors by penetrating authors' lives and knowing as much about them as possible.

The pendulum swings back and forth between critical focus on the "work" and the "life." To paraphrase the first two lines of Yeats' poem "The Choice," sometimes literary critics are forced to choose the life or the work. Whatever the utility or eventual outcome of this controversy, each side in the debate presumes that one knows whom the author is — that the author is in fact identifiable. In the case of Shakespeare's works, however, this is a problem. We have the works — the plays and poems — attributed by tradition to one Shakespeare. But — aye, there's the rub — we are, if we are candid with ourselves, not absolutely sure who "Shakespeare" really was. We simply do not know for certain who wrote Shakespeare's works.

This uncertainty over Shakespeare's true identity has fueled the authorship debate — a centuries-old controversy of varying interest and intensity. Some people, de facto followers of the New Critics, do not care that much who wrote the Shakespeare plays. For them, the works themselves are all that matter, and echoing the Bard, say in effect that an author by any other name would write as sweet. However, for many others — those who believe in the premise of intellectual biography — the authorship debate is crucial, endlessly fascinating, and bears heavily on the meaning of the works themselves. We will know the plays better and understand and appreciate them more, some say, if we know about the life of the person who wrote them. Knowledge of events in the life of the author may facilitate a more accurate interpretation of the meaning of particular works.

"No one would argue today," writes Joseph Epstein in *Plausible Prejudices*, "that you should not study both the artist and his work." Adds Epstein, "It is no longer possible, then, to ignore the importance of biography to literary study." At the same time, we should be wary of treating literary works merely as windows through which a writer's life can be viewed. We should not assume that authors deploy their fiction as evidence for biography.

Because of the uncertainty of authorship regarding Shakespeare's works, we must here reverse the premise of intellectual biography. Since we are not absolutely positive who wrote the works, we cannot use the life to illuminate the plays. Rather, we must work backward, using the plays to illuminate the life and studying what "Shakespeare" wrote for whatever light it might shed on his life in order to discover the author. In other words, we can closely read the plays and poems to see if they yield clues to the identity of their author.

SHAKESPEARE AND THE LAW

In this reversed search process, an important clue may lie in the many legal themes and references embedded in Shakespeare's plays. In a manner and with a number impossible to ignore, the plays constantly and impressively refer to the law. The basic action of some plays, such as *The Merchant of Venice, Measure for Measure,* and *The Winter's Tale* turns on the outcome of a legal proceeding. Twenty of Shakespeare's plays have trial scenes. Several other plays have many comments on the problems of law, lawyers, revenge, equity, government, the nature of the state, the nature and transfer of power, inheritance, and contracts.

Thus, the plays on their face reflect much knowledge of legal intricacies. Legal themes of one kind or another are pervasive. And woven throughout, like barbed wire sewn into a tapestry, are cutting observations about law and lawyers, each glinting shard designed to draw just a little blood from the legal profession. Four hundred years later, the profession is still reeling — and the rest of society is still rollicking — at the memorable line, "The first thing we do, let's kill all the lawyers."

Simply put, law is absolutely essential to our understanding and interpretation of Shakespeare's works.

DID SHAKESPEARE HAVE LEGAL TRAINING?

So let us begin with hope, courage, and a dash of skepticism to apply our reverse premise to Shakespeare's works. The number and intricacies of the legal themes and references in Shakespeare's works inform our inquiry, or at least supply some useful hypotheses. The abundance of legal references in Shakespeare's works makes us wonder. They provide a launching pad for useful inferences about their creator. We start to contemplate how and why this fellow Shakespeare, whoever he was, came to use the law the way he did in his writings. What might the large amount of law in Shakespeare's writing tell us about the author himself, his life, and his background?

Two possible basic inferences quickly come to mind. On one hand, the author's legal knowledge could imply legal training or experience. The legal knowledge in the works might seem too detailed and too accurate for anyone without formal legal training or considerable professional experience. This inference gave rise to the notion that only a lawyer could have been the true author. For a long time Francis Bacon was the leading lawyer candidate for this title, but now de Vere, the hero of "Anonymous," seems to occupy that spot. Today's supporters of de Vere are organized and quite zealous in their advocacy.

On the other hand, a second possibility is more congenial and less upsetting to those unwilling to concede that someone besides Shakespeare of Stratford was the author. That possibility is that Shakespeare may have acquired his impressive legal knowledge by working as a lawyer's clerk or court clerk. Indeed, the law clerk theme is a familiar suggestion and has found several adherents. They claim that Shakespeare served this clerkship between 1584 and 1595, a decade for which almost nothing is known of Shakespeare's life, making refutation difficult. This void in Shakespeare's biography, known as the "Lost Years," has become a wishing well for Shakespeare commentators. Legends about Shakespeare's life have found a convenient home in this biographical black hole because no one can prove the contrary beyond a reasonable doubt.

In either event, both of these inferences — lawyer or law clerk — have something in common. They both build on the hypothesis that the presence of so much law in Shakespeare's writing implies that the author must have had serious and professional legal training. The fundamental logic is really quite straightforward. The plays contain a vast number of legal references that are always so apt, precise, and accurate that they could have been written only by someone intimately familiar with the law from long training and practical experience. Therefore, the working assumption emerges that Shakespeare was somehow trained in the law, and he had, as Hamlet says in the gravedigger scene, the "skull of a lawyer."

Passionate debate has swirled for centuries around Shakespeare's supposed legal training. It began in the 1790s with a London barrister,

Edmund Malone, who wrote a biographical introduction to the plays in which he first floated the lawyer/law clerk theory. Ever since, many others — mostly lawyers — have joined the fray, both for and against the theory. Leaders of the English bar, including eminent judges, have chimed in. American scholars down to the present have added their voices. With so many strong-minded and opinionated participants, it is perhaps not surprising that the scholarly jury is far from unanimous either way.

But even American commentators, who as a matter of national culture and literary heritage should know better, have scanted our own Mark Twain's evidence on the issue. W. Michael Knight, author of *Shakespeare's Hidden Life: Shakespeare at the Law, 1585-1595*, thinks Shakespeare had some kind of legal career, and believes scholarship in this area "should carefully but fearlessly weigh the pros and cons of new documentary evidence" and should not be "timid" or "reluctant." That is precisely what we need to do with Twain's virtually unknown evidence, which is new in the sense of being newly appreciated.

Twain testified twice on the issue, once in an essay near the end of his life dealing specifically with the authorship issue and once on an earlier occasion, more obliquely but perhaps more tellingly, in his introduction to his novel *Pudd'nhead Wilson*, a precursor to today's legal thrillers. Taking our cue from Knight, we should "carefully but fearlessly" look at Mark Twain's evidence without being "timid" or "reluctant."

TWAIN'S 1909 ESSAY

Unfortunately, Twain's essay on Shakespeare's identity is little known and even less cited. This neglect is a huge mistake because Twain's evidence represents his mature reflections, the ripe fruits of a lifetime of thinking on the issue. It is, in some ways, the homage of one great writer, fully aware of his own unique stature, to another; America's best and best-loved author commenting on Britain's best and best-loved author — two literary heroes of the English-speaking peoples.

Perhaps with a touch of envy, Twain notes that Shakespeare's works, "will endure until the last sun goes down." But any envy that Twain felt might have slightly lessened had he lived to read Ernest Hemingway's famous comment in *Green Hills of Africa* that, "All modern American literature comes from one book by Mark Twain called *Huckleberry Finn*.

It's the best book we've had. All American writing comes from that. There was nothing before. There has been nothing since."

Surprisingly, then, one scours the authorship debate literature in vain for anything more than a rare passing reference to Twain's comments on Shakespeare's identity, let alone serious analysis and consideration of them. Even James Shapiro's 2010 *Contested Will*, drawing on an earlier version of this chapter that I published in 2004, does not go nearly far enough.

Twain's lively evidence took the form of a fifty-page essay entitled *Is Shakespeare Dead?* Originally meant for odd reasons to be part of his sprawling (and rambling) autobiography, the essay was first published as a book — Twain's last published book — in April 1909, shortly before Twain's death at age seventy-five. It does not resemble what we think of today as academic writing. Instead, it reads like an aggressive lawyer's brief, polemical in style with a take-no-prisoners tone, though at times it is wordy and wandering. As one would expect from Mark Twain, it is vibrant, improvised, irreverent, accessible, and anything but dry or dense. Like its author — a man of strong opinions — the essay is bold, direct, impatient, strident, restless. At the same time, it is curious, provocative, stimulating, passionate, sarcastically humorous, charming, memorably written, and, above all, entertaining. In a word, the essay is vintage Mark Twain.

"Excited" by a book entitled *The Shakespeare Problem Restated* by George Greenwood, which he received as a gift from a friend in England, Twain composed *Is Shakespeare Dead?* to air his own long gestating thoughts on the authorship debate. He basically agrees with Greenwood's conclusion that the Stratford Shakespeare was not capable of writing the works and that Shakespeare was a practicing lawyer. Yet how Twain arrives at his conclusion — his intellectual journey, his process of mind — is ever so interesting.

Knowing that he was swimming against a powerful tide, Twain needed a powerful stroke and, as usual, relied heavily on sarcasm and humor. Like Aristophanes and Bernard Shaw, Twain often wrapped his most serious points in humor. "Against the assault of laughter," wrote Twain in *The Mysterious Stranger*, "nothing stands." Indeed, Twain even borrows a technique from Mark Antony's funeral oration in *Julius Caesar*. Like Antony, Twain at times speaks by subtle and clever indirection. He sometimes says one thing, but means precisely the contrary. He uses ironic repetition to good effect.

He complains, for example, that the Stratfordians call their critics horrible and unpleasant names. But Twain purports to decline to stoop to that level. "I will not apply injurious epithets to them," Twain promises, appearing to meekly turn the other cheek, because "[s]uch violations of courtesy," he protests, are "repugnant to my nature and dignity." Instead Twain, seeming to take the high road, declares he will call Stratfordians only by "names of limited reverence—names merely descriptive, never unkind, [and] never offensive, never tainted by harsh feeling." He will, like a gentleman, use "terms reflecting [his] disapproval," but "without malice [and] without venom."

Twain, the great comic, is only setting us up. His pledge to avoid name-calling is, like the witches' prophecies to Macbeth, a promise to the ear, broken to the hope. As any good storyteller — and Twain was that if nothing else — he knows that timing is everything. In actuality, his kindest labels for his adversaries are "cults," "upholders" of the "Stratford-Shakespeare superstition" and the "Stratford myth." Immediately after telling us he is above relying on epithets, Twain abruptly pulls the string and proceeds to dub his opponents "slaves," "thugs," "Stratfordolaters," "troglodytes" and "criminals." His final blow makes modern academic debates seem tame indeed by comparison. "Taught by the methods found effective in extinguishing earlier offenders by the Inquisition, of holy memory," Twain mock threatens, "I shall know how to quiet" the Stratfordians.

Twain tries to quiet the Stratfordians by finding the "master key" to the authorship controversy. As a result of the huge number and particular types of legal references in the plays, Twain distills the debate to this: "If I had under my superintendence a controversy to decide whether Shakespeare wrote Shakespeare or not, I believe I would place before the debaters only the one question, *Was Shakespeare ever a practicing lawyer?* and leave everything else out." A few pages later, he repeats that he would "narrow the matter down to a single question . . . *Was the author of Shakespeare's Works a lawyer?* — a lawyer deeply read and of limitless experience?" Twain adds that he would "stand or fall, win or lose, by the verdict rendered by the jury upon that simple question." If the answer is "Yes," then he would "feel quite convinced that the Stratford Shakespeare . . . did not write the works."

"Yes" is how Twain resoundingly and unequivocally answers the key question he posed. The author of Shakespeare's works was a lawyer, says Twain. To come to this conclusion, Twain relies on what he calls "expert testimony." He quotes nine pages from Greenwood's book that in turn quote several eminent English judges and lawyers who state that Shakespeare must have been a practicing lawyer. Twain describes these judges and lawyers as "illustrious experts of unimpeachable competency" and "unchallengeable authority" and describes their evidence as "great testimony." He regards this "testimony" as "so strong . . . so authoritative . . . that it quite convinces me that the man who wrote Shakespeare's Works knew all about law and lawyers. Also that that man could not have been the Stratford Shakespeare — and *wasn't*."

Twain rejects all alternative theories for lack of evidence. He stresses that very few actual facts are known about Shakespeare and that everything else is made of "guesses, inferences, theories, [and] conjectures." He compares the common image of Shakespeare to a museum reconstruction of a dinosaur: "nine bones and six-hundred barrels of plaster of Paris." Shakespeare, Twain points out, was not regarded as a celebrity in Stratford. His death, unlike what happened when "distinguished literary folk of Shakespeare's time passed from life . . . was not an event . . . made no stir, [and] attracted no attention."

The lack of contemporary hometown interest in Shakespeare leads Twain to do what few among us or in history would be bold enough to dare. With outsized bravado, he compares himself to Shakespeare. "If Shakespeare had really been celebrated, like me," writes Twain modestly, "Stratford could have told things about him; and if my experience goes for anything, they'd have done it." According to Twain, "nobody seems to have been interested" in Shakespeare for seven years after his death, until Ben Jonson's Introduction to the First Folio in 1623. And sixty years after his death, villagers in Stratford could recall nothing about Shakespeare.

He specifically dismisses explanations about how the Stratford Shakespeare could have become learned in the law. Twain brushes aside the law clerk theory as mere "surmise." For Twain, "there is no evidence — and not even tradition — that the young Shakespeare was ever clerk of a law-court." Nor is there any evidence to Twain's mind that young Shakespeare accumulated his legal knowledge by reading law books or "by picking up lawyer-talk and the rest of it through loitering about the law-courts and listening." More "surmise," says Twain, "merely a couple of chunks of plaster of Paris."

If the man from Stratford was not the author, Twain asks, "Who did write these works, then?" He answers his own question with feigned humility: "I wish I knew." He adds, "Did Francis Bacon write Shakespeare's Works? Nobody knows." Despite this disclaimer, Twain proceeds to unveil the evidence in favor of Bacon, particularly Bacon's legal, literary and other abilities and accomplishments, which leads Twain to "strongly suspect[]" that Bacon wrote Shakespeare under a pen name.

Ultimately, however, Twain assumes an agnostic stance and he does so because of a failure of proof. He concludes, "We cannot say we *know* a thing when that thing has not been proved. *Know* is too strong a word to use when the evidence is not final and absolutely conclusive." That is Mark Twain's inconclusive final verdict, expressed in legal terms, in his 1909 essay on Shakespeare's identity.

MARK TWAIN EFFECTIVELY CROSS-EXAMINES

The most enchanting, most original, and most lawyerly aspect of Twain's neglected essay is a particularly effective cross-examination to drive home his main point. It is a cross-examination that, if Twain is to be believed, he actually conducted as a young man. It is instructive both on the authorship question and as an example of good courtroom technique. It is the high point in Twain's 1909 essay, especially to a lawyer.

Near the beginning of his essay, Twain describes an incident from his young adulthood in which, as a pilot-apprentice, he tried to convince a Mississippi riverboat "pilot master" — who was "an idolater of Shakespeare" — that Shakespeare could not have written Shakespeare. The two of them, apprentice Twain and "this Shakespeare-adoring Mississippi pilot," argued for "months" about this in 1857 or 1858. The pilot talked about it "in the morning watch, the middle watch, and dog watch; and probably kept it going in his sleep." They discussed it "all through thirteen hundred miles of river four times traversed in every thirty-five days." The pilot bought the literature on the topic as soon as it came out. He had an "argumentative disposition," expressing his opinions "with heat, with energy, [and] with violence."

This word picture alone is stunning, and is a vision worth lingering over for a moment. Shakespeare on the Mississippi . . . what a wonderful and captivating portrait of nineteenth-century America and the reading habits of a free and enlightened people! Here we have two self-taught (Twain left school at twelve when his father died), self-made midwesterners, one a young man in his early twenties, the other a mature pilot. They were the only two people on a Mississippi riverboat, and they heatedly argued with each other for months about who wrote Shakespeare, as they made round trips back and forth on the River. The inspiring and emblematic image of this debate is almost too extraordinary for the mind's eye, as the scene symbolizes and describes the broadly democratic, post-Jacksonian, egalitarian, American attitude toward culture, a true democracy of readers rising up against an aristocracy of scholars and critics.

This 1909 essay was not the first time Twain had written about people reading to each other and talking Shakespeare while traveling down the Mississippi. The debate scene in Twain's essay reminds us of some of the most unforgettable scenes in *Huckleberry Finn*. Huck, you will recall, was an avid reader, and he would read aloud to Jim and talk about what he was reading. "I read considerable to Jim about kings and dukes and earls and such, and how gaudy they dressed, and how much style they put on, and called each other your majesty, and your grace, and your lordship, and so on, 'stead of mister; and Jim's eyes bugged out, and he was interested."

Huck's reading aloud about royalty comes to comic life when Huck and Jim are joined on their raft by two fast-talking charlatans who call themselves the Duke of Bridgewater and the King of France. To raise some quick cash, the two mountebanks, while on the raft, come up with the idea of performing in little riverbank towns a few scenes from *Romeo and Juliet*, *Richard III*, and *Hamlet*. The king and duke use the raft to rehearse and while doing so, the king falls overboard as they practice a sword fight. The duke rehearses something that is supposed to be Hamlet's "to be or not to be" soliloquy, but in fact combines bits and pieces from several plays in a riotous and nonsensical fashion. It is impossible to read Twain's 1909 essay without calling to mind these scenes from *Huckleberry Finn*.

To a certain extent, then, Twain's 1909 essay on Shakespeare has something in common with Twain's greatest book. The debaters on the riverboat in the later Shakespeare essay also are not highborn, expensively educated Englishmen or professors, but, rather, ordinary working people on this side of the Atlantic. They are passionately interested in the life of the mind even as they go about their daily work and try to earn a living on the edge of the frontier. Unlike Huck and Jim, Twain and the pilot do not find the "great Mississippi, the majestic, the magnificent Mississippi" a refuge or an escape from civilization, except in the sense of escaping the distractions of civilization that would otherwise have interfered with their civilized debate. After all, the Mississippi was a real highway; all life, social and economic, centered there.

For Twain and the pilot, travelling the river is partly an intellectual exercise and struggle. They argue about the ideas of the civilized men and women on shore. For the two of them, Shakespeare was not some remote, faraway topic, or the exclusive property of elitist academics. Instead, Shakespeare belonged to everyone, including amateurs like themselves (an encouraging attitude that persists to this day). Is not such a vision a magnificent tribute to admirable American concepts of widespread access to art, of democracy of the mind? Reading Twain's essay, we can almost imagine what that invigorating atmosphere, the democratic spirit of the times, was like.

This bracing nineteenth-century atmosphere caught the eye of foreign visitors to this country. The most famous and most influential was the young, aristocratic Frenchman Alexis de Tocqueville, who came here in the 1830s to find out why attempts to establish democracy in France had failed while the American Revolution had produced a stable democratic republic. One reason Tocqueville discovered was Americans' widespread literacy and interest in reading.

In his masterpiece *Democracy in America*, Tocqueville includes a perceptive chapter on "The Influences of Democracy on Language and Literature," which sets the scene nicely. Tocqueville there says America has produced an "ever-increasing crowd of readers" and that literature reaches "into the recesses of the forests of the New World." To demonstrate his generalization and underline Shakespeare's popular appeal in America, Tocqueville writes, "There is hardly a pioneer's hut which does not contain a few odd volumes of Shakespeare." Tocqueville saw that, despite the hardships of the frontier, a "large number of persons are nevertheless to be found there who take an interest in the productions of the mind, and who make them, if not the study of their lives, at least the charm of their leisure hours."

Of course this is exactly what Twain and the master pilot were doing. They were using their leisure hours, in Tocqueville's words, to "taste occasionally and by stealth the pleasures of the mind." Even if those pleasures "do not constitute the principal charm of their lives," observes Tocqueville, "they are considered as a transient and necessary recreation amid the serious labors of life." So, we should pay attention to the wise French nobleman and, as he instructs, "Let us transport ourselves into the midst of a democracy, not unprepared by ancient tradition and present culture to partake in the pleasures of the mind." Return with us now to that extraordinary debate between Mark Twain and the riverboat pilot over who wrote Shakespeare.

While on watch, the pilot would read Shakespeare to Twain, who was steering. The pilot, however, did not read without interruption, as "he constantly injected commands" about Twain's steering. According to Twain, the result was a combination of Shakespearean text and "explosive interlardings" about how to steer a steamboat.

Twain "got the best of [the pilot] only once." Twain wanted to settle an argument with the pilot over how Shakespeare knew so much about "the laws, and the law-courts, and law-proceedings, and lawyer-talk, and lawyer-ways." So, like a good lawyer, he "prepared" himself and devised a clever plan that would have made Edward Bennett Williams proud.

Twain wrote out a passage from Shakespeare and "riddled it with [the pilot's] wild steamboatful interlardings." Then he asked the pilot to read it aloud, which the flattered pilot did with gusto. About a week after the dramatic reading, the pilot and Twain argued about whether Shakespeare knew enough law to write the plays attributed to him. As Twain anticipated from past discussions, the pilot insisted that Shakespeare learned his law from reading books, which allowed Twain to spring his cross-examination trap.

Twain explained his theory:

> [A] man can't handle glibly and easily and comfortably and successfully the argot of a trade at which he has not personally served. He will make mistakes; he will not, and cannot, get the trade-phrasings precisely and exactly right; and the moment he departs, by even a shade, from a common tradeform, the reader who has served that trade will know the writer *hasn't*.

But the pilot was unconvinced. He argued that a man could learn the language of any trade by careful reading and studying. Then Twain demonstrated how the pilot discovered the truth for himself. As Twain recalled the exchange,

[W]hen [he] got [the pilot] to read again the passage from Shakespeare with the interlardings, he perceived, himself, that books couldn't teach a student a bewildering multitude of pilot-phrases so thoroughly and perfectly that he could talk them off in book and play or conversation and make no mistake that a pilot would not immediately discover.

Twain considered the episode to be a "triumph."

This "triumph" dramatizes the core and the real essence of Twain's views on who wrote Shakespeare. Twain stresses, in his essay, that a layperson simply could not write about the law the way Shakespeare did and that a layperson would be bound to make mistakes. He uses two other literary examples to support his case. Recalling his own experience as a miner, Twain swears he can tell the difference between phoney mining camp dialogue in his rival Bret Harte's stories and the real thing based on long practical experience from having "served that trade." By contrast, he cites Richard Henry Dana, Jr., author of *Two Years Before the Mast*, for "sailor-talk [that] flows from his pen with the sure touch and the ease and confidence of a person who has *lived* what he is talking about, not gathered it from books and random listenings."

As a writer, Twain knew that actual experience was important. In the essay, Twain explains that experience "is an author's most valuable asset." Bearing in mind his own life, he states that "experience is the thing that puts the muscle and the breath and the warm blood into the book he writes." Given Twain's strong feeling about the crucial importance of experience, it is not hard to understand how he came to his conclusion about Shakespeare's identity. It is his major original contribution in the essay. When he talks about experience, he is not being funny. He is serious and should not be ignored.

The real question, however, is not whether Twain is serious, but whether he is correct in concluding that only a practicing lawyer could have written Shakespeare's works. Unlike Twain's pilot master, we have to approach this question without an "argumentative disposition," although we are allowed to use some "heat" and "energy" but no "violence." Before his 1909 essay, Twain himself may have actually answered the question in the negative.

TWAIN'S 1894 "WHISPER": A PRIOR
INCONSISTENT STATEMENT

For a realistic picture, we need to look not only at what Twain says in his essay on Shakespeare — no matter how beguilingly and entertainingly — but also at what he actually does in writing about law. Intellectual consistency was not Twain's strong suit. Like a lawyer, he deals with the particular issue before him, even if what he says on one occasion contradicts what he says on another. Twain marshals the arguments sufficient for the moment. He is not a system-builder.

A telling example of such inconsistency is the discrepancy between, on one hand, Twain's so-called "proof" that Shakespeare's works were not written by the Stratford Shakespeare and, on the other, Twain's contrary statements and performance fifteen years earlier. That prior 1894 evidence too is an important, if inconsistent, part of Twain's testimony. An adversary cross-examiner, one of Twain's troglodyte "Stratfordolaters," might even think of using it as a prior inconsistent statement to try to impeach Twain's credibility and discredit his views on the authorship issue.

As for his own argument that someone must be a lawyer to write about the law without error, Twain himself provides an important and overlooked rebuttal. His book *Pudd'nhead Wilson*, written in 1894, is a noteworthy legal novel about a "nice guy" lawyer in a small town whose lifelong hobby of fingerprinting eventually places him in the legal limelight. Twain's book has trial scenes, involves specialized knowledge, and otherwise displays actual familiarity with legal procedures. *Pudd'nhead Wilson* became a significant model for later American depictions of the legal profession.

Thus, Twain himself seriously undercuts the homespun cleverness of the cross-examination that he played on his steamboat pilot master. With *Pudd'nhead Wilson*, Twain shows that a non-lawyer can indeed write knowledgeably and accurately about legal technicalities. In that book, Twain writes exhaustively about law and legal proceedings. Shakespeare and Twain (along with Melville and Dickens) are brilliant non-lawyer storytellers who link their frequent legal themes to the way lawyers talk and write.

Pudd'nhead Wilson reveals deep, although unacknowledged, contradictions in Twain's stance on Shakespeare. Before the actual text of *Pudd'nhead Wilson* begins, Twain offers a brief "Whisper to the Reader" that must startle anyone who has read Twain's essay on Shakespeare. "A person who is ignorant of legal matters," begins Twain's Whisper, "is always liable to make mistakes when he tries to photograph a court scene with his pen." Based on this statement alone, there is no discrepancy between Twain's author's note to his 1894 novel and his position in his 1909 Shakespeare essay. In both writings, Twain simply observes that laypersons are inevitably going to make mistakes when writing about legal technicalities.

Then, however, Twain parts company with himself. What he next writes completely subverts his entire argument about Shakespeare's unfamiliarity with law. Continuing his introductory note to *Pudd'nhead Wilson*, Twain writes, "[A]nd so I was not willing to let the law chapters in this book go to press without first subjecting them to exhausting revision and correction by a trained barrister." And that is exactly what Twain does, contending that "[t]hese chapters are right, now, in every detail, for they were rewritten under the immediate eye" of a lawyer, who approved the revisions.

That's it! That's the answer! Or at least one of the answers. With those two sentences, Twain refutes Twain on the supposed need for Shakespeare to have been a lawyer. He supplies an alternative, a third hypothesis.

Why, we might justifiably ask, could Shakespeare not have done the same thing as Twain did, and submitted his legal allusions to a lawyer friend from the Inns of Court for vetting and correction? Why does Twain's 1909 essay deriding Shakespeare's ability to make legal references fail to mention his own simple method, relied on so successfully and so openly fifteen years earlier with *Pudd'nhead Wilson*, for ensuring the accuracy of a layperson's writing about the intricacies of the law? Why does Twain neither recognize the differences in his positions nor attempt to reconcile them?

Curiously, Twain's glaring contradiction has evaded comment by Shakespeare scholars. Like his contemporary Walt Whitman, Twain was large and contained multitudes, but that is hardly a clear and convincing explanation, nor a particularly satisfying one, for his so contradicting himself. The disparity between Twain's essay on Shakespeare and his "Whisper to the Reader" in *Pudd'nhead Wilson* opens a new line of argument. The "Whisper" is Twain on truth serum. Rather than shouting, joking, and carrying on as he usually does, Twain in the Whisper quietly confesses the truth about non-lawyers writing about law. He there speaks softly and honestly and openly, without artifice or humorous fireworks. Maybe that is why he calls it a "whisper." In this introductory comment, Twain helps point the way toward resolving the debate by practical experience — not the experience he referred to in his 1909 essay but rather the experience he actually demonstrates as a writer in *Pudd'nhead Wilson*.

LAWYERS' BIAS

Lawyers like me must be especially careful about the lawyer/law clerk theory of Shakespeare biography. We must be wary of imposing our wishes on the facts and disregarding our own professional training about how to look at evidence without bias. Our interpretation of the evidence may be affected by emotional, psychological, and professional factors. Twain notwithstanding, lawyers have been the most frequent and most vocal champions of the lawyer/law clerk theory. But behind the lawyer/law clerk theory may lie a thinly veiled subconscious or even unconscious triple-pronged conceit of the legal profession.

First, lawyers writing about Shakespeare who believe Shakespeare had a legal background may fall into the trap of identification and personal projection. Whoever writes about Shakespeare, it is often said, writes about himself or herself. Second, to conclude that Shakespeare was a lawyer is to extol the virtues of being a lawyer and to enhance self-esteem of lawyers by allowing them to feel a special kinship with Shakespeare's genius. Third, lawyers may think that no one but a lawyer (or one trained in the law) could write about the law.

In light of these potential sources of professional vanity, one becomes skeptical of the lawyers' arguments. If we at least know the motivation — the professional complacency that may underlie some of the arguments and attitudes — then we may more accurately evaluate what is said. Wishful thinking must be discounted when the facts so warrant, or we will see only what we want to see and that will be distorted. When lawyers' insecurities and objective reality clash, it is not reality that must yield. Above all, we must be clear eyed in looking at the evidence and even mere awareness of lawyers' self-interest in this matter helps us accomplish that.

The skepticism — or at least warning — arising from the unconscious professional motives behind the law clerk/lawyer hypothesis supplies a bracing backdrop for considering the evidence, including the evidence of non-lawyer Mark Twain. We need a healthy, probing, and questioning cast of mind — a mind like Mark Twain's most of the time — for a subject encrusted with received wisdom and too much deference to authority.

WEIGHING TWAIN'S EVIDENCE

Twain was well aware of the quixotic nature of his 1909 essay and the high burden of proof he would have to meet to "convince anybody that Shakespeare did not write Shakespeare's Works." Twain compares Shakespeare's Stratford identity to a childhood superstition. Twain argues that "it will never be possible" for "even the brightest mind" to examine "sincerely, dispassionately, and conscientiously any evidence or any circumstance which shall seem to cast a doubt upon the validity of that superstition." Twain thinks that our belief in who wrote Shakespeare is something we get "second hand." We do not "reason" it out "for ourselves." We have been taught to believe in Shakespeare's Stratford identity, "and love it and worship it, and refrain from examining it." Twain muses pessimistically: "[T]here is no evidence, howsoever clear and strong, that can persuade us to withdraw from it our loyalty and our devotion."

Let us now try, to put it in Twain's own words, to "sincerely, dispassionately, and conscientiously" examine all of Twain's evidence. Let us see if it is "clear and strong," and which way it points.

Neglect Explained

The first step in such an examination is to understand why Twain's 1909 essay, widely available in various collections, has been so neglected, indeed virtually ignored, by Shakespeare studies. Of course, the essay goes against conventional wisdom, which does not make for popularity; nevertheless other anti-Stratfordian tracts have received far more attention. Its language is coarse and colloquial, is far removed from academic writing, a trait not saved by the way that Twain's colloquial style breathes life into his other writings. In addition, it is not closely reasoned. Filled with sarcasm, humor, and irrelevant digressions, *Is Shakespeare Dead?* is simply not taken seriously.

Apart from non-academic style, the essay lacks originality. Except for the riverboat debate passages, it is derivative. Its conclusion depends almost entirely on the correctness of the patchwork of undigested quotations by the "expert" witnesses in Greenwood's book about the legal knowledge in Shakespeare's works. In fact, Greenwood's London publishers even charged Twain at the time with plagiarizing from Greenwood's book and threatened to ban Twain's book in Great Britain. Accused of being a literary pirate, Twain insisted he had added a footnote in which he gave full credit to both author and publishers, but that the footnote was inadvertently lost in the printing.

In any event, "expert" testimony like that quoted by Twain tends to intimidate and overwhelm lawyers as well as non-lawyers. If leaders of the bar, who are presumably better able to evaluate such things, certify that Shakespeare had unusually extensive and preternaturally accurate knowledge of law, who are we to disagree? Deference to Shakespeare's legal profundity begins to look like automatic submission to authority. The argument from authority, often a compelling argument for many people, has special attraction for many lawyers who are prone by training and mind-set to defer to precedent.

But, as Montaigne long ago stressed in his essay on education, we must learn to think for ourselves. A person must "sift everything, and take nothing into his head on authority or trust. . . . Let their various opinions be put before him; he will choose between them if he can, if not, he will remain in doubt."

The real question, then, is not whether Twain's essay is original, but rather, is it persuasive? "Not very" is the most intellectually honest answer we can give. The core problem is that Twain, usually a great skeptic, is not nearly skeptical enough of the experts' pronouncements regarding Shakespeare's legal knowledge. To claim that the plays reflect vast legal knowledge is not to prove anything about the legal training of the author of the plays. That kind of leap is just the type of surmising Twain finds so objectionable. According to Twain biographer and expert Charles Neider, "A skilled dialectician, using the kind of 'evidence' that Clemens here finds acceptable, could no doubt prove that Clemens could not have written most of his books, having been too uneducated, too etcetera, to have done so."

Evidentiary Objections

When a federal appeals court noted in 1995 that some disciplines "have the courtroom as a principal theatre of operations," it probably did not have Shakespeare's plays in mind.* Yet Twain's heavy reliance on "expert testimony" and his invitation to examine the "evidence" entitle us, as a thought experiment, to invoke some real rules of evidence.

Hearsay. A preliminary objection to Twain's parade of expert witnesses is that their testimony is hearsay. Twain merely quotes Greenwood's book, which in turn quotes the so-called authorities. It is then double hearsay — hearsay within hearsay — and it is not subject to cross-examination. Therefore, one might object at the outset.

However, the hearsay objection to Twain's expert testimony might not be sustained. The nineteenth-century experts are unavailable either because of death or because they cannot be made to attend by process or other reasonable means. But one might regard their published opinions as "former testimony," which is not excludable as hearsay even if the witnesses themselves are unavailable. Therefore, the hearsay objection might or might not succeed, but the inability to cross-examine Twain's experts remains a severe handicap.

Unreliability. A more substantial objection exists. Under the Supreme Court's important 1995 decision in *Daubert v. Merrill Dow Pharmaceuticals, Inc.*, trial judges have the responsibility of acting as gatekeepers to exclude unreliable expert testimony, which includes all expert testimony, not just testimony based in science. The initial question in evaluating this objection becomes whether Twain's expert evidence is reliable and helpful. One factor relevant in determining whether expert testimony is sufficiently reliable is whether the experts have adequately accounted for obvious alternative explanations. This factor is the greatest weakness of Twain's expert testimony.

Obvious alternative explanations exist. Shakespeare's knowledge of law and his use of legal allusions were far from unusual among Elizabethan playwrights. Elizabethan England was enthralled by law, litigation was common, and law was a national preoccupation. Thus, it is understandable that legal allusions and themes would appear in Shakespeare's works. Many of Shakespeare's expressions, in modern times confined to legal usage, were in popular use in Shakespeare's day

---

* Daubert v. Merrill Dow Pharm., Inc., 43 F.3d 1311, 1317 n.5 (9th Cir. 1995).

as clichés and do not imply a special acquaintance with the law. Nor is it hard to believe that a voracious reader such as Shakespeare would not, in an era so marked by legal influence, have read some law books even if he never entertained the idea of practicing as a lawyer. He also likely gleaned legal expressions from his historical sources.

In his 1909 essay Twain forgets that Shakespeare lived and worked in an atmosphere permeated by law. The Inns of Court were a central part of Shakespeare's and London's existence. He had friends and acquaintances who were lawyers. No doubt he attended court cases as a spectator. Shakespeare and his family were involved in a variety of legal proceedings. He employed and dealt with attorneys. All this gave him a working knowledge of the law.

THE PROOF OF THE PUDD'N

Twain's evidence in his 1909 essay also overlooks the alternative explanation he himself gave in *Pudd'nhead Wilson*. Even though *Pudd'nhead Wilson* does not explicitly address the Shakespeare authorship question, Twain's legal novel implicitly weighs in on the issue. That novel, along with many examples of later legal fiction and non-fiction, demonstrates that it is possible and indeed fairly common for non-lawyers, like Twain, to write intelligently about the law. As Professor Yoshino points out, "I believe Shakespeare knew a lot about the law, but only as a by-product of knowing a lot about everything."

Dickens's *Bleak House, David Copperfield,* and *Great Expectations* contain extended discussions of law cases, lawyers, the practice of law, and legal subjects. Twentieth-century examples include Theodore Dreiser's *An American Tragedy*, Albert Camus's *The Stranger*, Bernard Malamud's *The Fixer*, Tom Wolfe's *Bonfire of the Vanities*, Herman Wouk's *Caine Mutiny*, Leon Uris's *QB VII*, and William Gaddis's *A Frolic of His Own*. In the non-fiction realm, two of the finest books about American law — *Simple Justice* by Richard Kluger and *Gideon's Trumpet* by Anthony Lewis — were written by non-lawyers. A slew of popular true crime books — which almost always describe court trials — and legal biographies have come from the pens and personal computers of non-lawyers.

If others less gifted than Shakespeare have written about the law, so too could Shakespeare have done it. It is difficult to maintain that only a lawyer or person with legal training could write a book about law. An author need not be a member of the guild to write about it with discernment and understanding.

Creative writers write not only from experience but also from their imagination. They make things up. That is in part why their work product is called fiction. It slights the achievement of imaginative literature to claim that a writer can write only out of what happens in his or her own life. Attempts to correlate too closely the events or acquaintances of an author's life with his or her creative writing run the risk of reducing the vital role of an author's imagination almost out of existence.

And what authors cannot make up, they can research. Virtually every author does this. Even one of the classic pro-Oxfordian and anti-Stratfordian books — *"Shakespeare" Identified* by J. Thomas Looney — concluded in 1920 that "it is open to question whether [for example, the law in Shakespeare] is the law of a professional lawyer, or that of an intelligent man who had a fair amount of important business to transact with lawyers, and was himself interested in the study of law as many laymen have been."

Twain's stress on actual experience may be misplaced or at least overdone. It may overlook a "gift" of great writers beyond their imagination, a gift for "picking up authentic details of anything," or "of assimilating other men's activities and shop talk as it were out of the air." Such a gift is "very valuable" and "has given substance to some major works of art." But it is a gift unrecognized by Twain. That writer's gift for picking up shop talk would blunt the effectiveness of Twain's entertaining cross-examination of his friend the riverboat pilot. It would shake Twain's premise that "a man can't handle . . . the argot of a trade at which he has not personally served."

Any sincere, dispassionate, and conscientious review of Twain's evidence on Shakespeare's identity must therefore go beyond *Is Shakespeare Dead?* In such an evaluation, one must examine the totality of his testimony, which includes *Pudd'nhead Wilson* as well as Twain's 1909 essay. This evidence embraces not only what Twain said in the introduction to *Pudd'nhead Wilson*, but also what he, a layman, accomplished in writing a legal novel. Placing Twain's essay and novel simultaneously in the scales thus raises more questions that it answers.

Of course, just because Twain had a lawyer vet the legal aspects of one novel does not mean Shakespeare did the same thing for any of his plays, let alone all of them. There is no evidence that Shakespeare did any such thing. Nor does the verification of occasional legal details, if it happened, necessarily explain Shakespeare's pervasive use of legal images, metaphors, and thinking. On close analysis, Twain's 1909 evidence in favor of the lawyer theory still starts to thin, while at the same time his 1894 testimony against the lawyer theory grows in cogency. Possibilities persist, but grave doubts remain after all.

A HUNG JURY?

In weighing all of Twain's evidence, including both the 1909 essay *Is Shakespeare Dead?* and the introduction to *Pudd'nhead Wilson*, the balance probably does not tip decidedly one way or the other for or against Shakespeare's formal legal training. Two fundamental failures of proof hobble Twain's advocacy of Shakespeare's formal legal training. First, as Twain explained in the "Whisper to Reader," it is unclear whether Shakespeare learned enough law to equip him to make legal references in his work. Second, the legal training advocates indulge themselves in much speculation. Absent hard evidence, Twain is engaging in the very "guesses, inferences, theories, [and] conjectures" that he forswears. These two flaws, together with common sense and the experience of modern non-lawyer authors writing about law, seriously dilute the evidence that Shakespeare was either a law clerk or a lawyer.

Although reasonable people do differ on the verdict, we should at least agree on the importance of Mark Twain's evidence. If the author of America's first undisputed literary masterpiece has thoughts on Shakespeare's identity, they are definitely worth our attention. His 1909 essay was meant to be taken seriously, and we should seriously consider it. The essay should be exhumed — the reports of its death (like that of its author) have been greatly exaggerated — and it should be widely studied and debated. It is both fascinating and vital because it reveals Twain's love of Shakespeare, it gives his considered views on who wrote Shakespeare, and it etches a significant portrait of the nineteenth-century American mind.

Equally important to the authorship question is *Pudd'nhead Wilson*. The book probably deserves even more attention than *Is Shakespeare Dead?* because its link to the authorship debate is by no means obvious. When Twain's 1909 essay is compared with his 1894 novel, the contrast is stark and cannot be ignored. *Pudd'nhead Wilson* places Twain's later essay in a whole new light. Analysis of *Pudd'nhead Wilson* adds to the authorship debate and increases our understanding of Twain. We should carefully consider evidence in both of his writings in the authorship debate.

It may be that in the end we can do no better than throw up our hands and admit, echoing Twain, "We do not know." Two scholars who studied the evidence seventy years ago, Paul Clarkson and Clyde Warren, wisely concluded in *The Law of Property in Shakespeare and Elizabethan Drama* that they could not "dogmatically" say that Shakespeare was not a lawyer, or that he had no legal education. The scholars were "agnostic: as a matter of biographical fact, we simply do not know." Even such careful scholars could state "categorically" that the evidence — the same evidence relied on by Twain — is "wholly insufficient to prove such a claim." Their tentative, modest, persuasive conclusion has a prudent and intellectually fresh and honest ring to it. It appears to represent the truth as we now know it.

Twain himself may have delivered the correct verdict on his own evidence, a verdict that merits repeating: "We cannot say we *know* a thing when that thing has not been proved. *Know* is too strong a word to use when the evidence is not final and absolutely conclusive."

Reversing the premise of intellectual biography and using Shakespeare's works to tell us about the author's life do yield results, albeit inconclusive ones. Even when a trial ends in a hung jury, however, the process of sifting through the evidence is itself helpful and enlightening. We learn more about the author. We learn more about his background and environment. We learn about the limits of literary evidence. And perhaps most important of all, we learn about ourselves, our beliefs, and our mental processes.

In any event, the wonderful riverboat debate, described so picturesquely by Mark Twain, continues in other forums, "with heat, [and] with energy," and will likely continue until, in Twain's words, "the last sun goes down" or, in the words of whoever wrote *Macbeth*, until the "crack of doom."

One of those other forums where debate continues over the authorship question and other questions about Shakespeare's plays is the moot court.

CHAPTER 2

Hamlet v. State of Denmark

Whoever wrote them, the plays of Shakespeare lend themselves to many different kinds and modes of analysis. One can read them, watch them, read about them, write about them, teach them, discuss them. A relatively new and surprisingly effective and entertaining method is to do moot courts based on Shakespeare plays.

A moot court is a mock trial or appeal. Moot courts have been familiar to all law students as part of their professional training in advocacy. In a tradition going back to the Inns of Court (residential law schools and professional clubs in London) and the Middle Ages, law schools have long required students to brief and argue cases in moot courts before visiting judges, teachers, practitioners, and fellow students. A Shakespeare moot court is a mock trial or appeal growing out of one of his plays.

Over the past two decades, such Shakespeare moot courts have become more common and ever more popular. Sponsored by law schools, bar associations, courts, and various Shakespeare societies, these moot courts consistently draw standing room only audiences composed of non-lawyers as well as lawyers. Leading newspapers have written about them.

One part of the attraction is a new way of thinking about great pieces of literature. Judging what Shakespeare's characters did in light of current American law may yield different insights than those gotten through traditional Shakespeare scholarship. Shakespeare moot courts educate.

Besides being educational, these moot courts make great theater.

27

They always feature the element and the lure of the unexpected. Moot courts are marked by spontaneity. Although the advocates may submit written briefs, the action is unscripted. One never knows what questions the judges will ask or what answers the advocates will give. A moot court puts a premium on thinking on one's feet. As a result, Shakespeare moot courts are almost a new genre or art form.

This new art form can also be fun. Shakespeare moot courts are often leavened with humor. The legal issues in Shakespeare's plays can be argued about in lighthearted ways that bring knowing smiles to the faces of onlookers. Sometimes such levity drives home a jurisprudential or dramatic point better than abstract or technical argument. We saw this effect with Mark Twain's analysis of the authorship debate. And we see it again and again in Shakespeare moot courts.

The ground rules for such moot courts are usually few and simple. For the most part, the text of the play provides the facts, that is, the record on appeal, although some adjustment may be necessary (*e.g.,* Hamlet does not die at the end of his play and can therefore stand trial). Similarly, where the play's text is ambiguous or silent, an advocate may use his or her imagination to fill in between the lines, to create certain facts. The legal briefs prepared by the advocates are usually much, much shorter than those that would be filed in a real court case, and often are distributed to the audience as it is seated for the performance.

The record on appeal can in a sense be live too. Relevant scenes from the play at issue are sometimes performed right before the moot court begins. For example, moot courts based on *The Merchant of Venice* have had actors perform both the scene in which Shylock and Antonio form their contract and the trial scene. This way the audience is entertainingly reminded of the basic facts.

Ruling on these Shakespeare moot courts are panels of judges. Although there is no magic number, the panels I have seen range from three to seven judges. The moot court judges themselves are actual judges or lawyers or Shakespeare experts or enthusiasts. The composition of these moot court benches often produces sharp questioning of the advocates.

What law should govern these Shakespeare moot courts is debatable. One might want to use the law of Shakespeare's time and place, or the time and place of the action in a particular play. But such legal rules are not easy to find, as well as being unfamiliar, out of date, and of such interest only to scholars and antiquarians. Much more useful, for a host of reasons, is our current American law. Relying on our contemporary law adds new dimensions to it and to the plays.

I have been lucky enough to be invited to be an advocate in several Shakespeare moot courts. Over the years I have both defended Hamlet and later prosecuted him, represented Shylock and in another moot court represented his nemesis Antonio, and once represented King Lear and Cordelia in an effort to recover the gifts given to Goneril and Regan when Lear arguably lacked the required mental capacity. All of these moot courts were wonderful, stimulating, unforgettable experiences.

Included here are actual briefs from moot courts based on two of Shakespeare's most famous plays, *Hamlet* and *The Merchant of Venice*. For each play, I ended up doing briefs for both sides because in one moot court I represented Hamlet, and in another the State of Denmark; in one I represented Shylock, and in another Antonio. That way, I had the rare opportunity to argue both sides of each case. What more could a lawyer hope for?

ROYAL DANISH COURT OF APPEALS
FOR THE ELSINORE CIRCUIT

————————————————————— X

STATE OF DENMARK,   :

        Appellee,   :

       - against -   :

HAMLET, PRINCE OF DENMARK, :

        Appellant.   :

————————————————————— X

BRIEF OF APPELLANT HAMLET*

Only rarely — once every four-hundred years or so — does a criminal case come along so riddled with interesting error as this one. This is an appeal from six homicide convictions: five for second degree murder (Laertes, Claudius, Polonius, and Rosencrantz and Guildenstern), N.Y. Penal Law § 125.25, and one for second degree manslaughter (Ophelia), N.Y. Penal Law § 125.15. On reexamining the judgment below, the Court, like one of the gravediggers who testified at trial, should ask, "But is this law?" (*Hamlet*, 5.1.20). The answer is "no," and each conviction should be reversed.

SINCE HAMLET SUFFERED FROM DIMINISHED MENTAL CAPACITY, SUCH LACK OF CULPABILITY REQUIRES REVERSAL ON ALL COUNTS

At trial appellant proved two defenses involving lack of culpability. First, he showed that at the time of the conduct alleged, as a result of mental disease or defect, he lacked substantial capacity to know or appreciate either (a) the nature and consequences of such conduct, or (b) that such conduct was wrong. *See* N.Y. Penal Law § 30.05. Second,

———————

*   Submitted for a moot court in 1994 at the New York City Bar association.

30

defendant at the very least met the lesser standard of proving that he acted under the influence of extreme emotional disturbance for which there was a reasonable explanation or excuse from the defendant's point of view. N.Y. Penal Law § 125.25. Mental disease or defect is a complete defense to all charges, and emotional disturbance is a defense to second degree murder and a mitigating factor for lesser offenses.

Appellant's mind was so disturbed and delusional that, as many witnesses observed, he talked irrationally, believed he saw and spoke to a ghost, and even explained that it was the ghost who told him to kill Claudius. Long referred to by the press as "the melancholy Dane," appellant, who testified at trial that he was at home recovering from a difficult and stressful year of studying law at Wittenberg University, was thrown further off balance and indeed grief stricken and severely depressed by his father's murder, his mother's quick marriage to the murderer— appellant's own uncle — and Ophelia's neglect of appellant's love. His emotional strain caused him to swing wildly between paralytic inaction and manic action. He even became suicidal.

The irrationality of such behavior hardly went unnoticed. Several of the decedents themselves had on a number of occasions called appellant "mad" and his actions "lunacy." Even Hamlet knew he was beset "with sore distraction." (5.2.176). "What I have done," Hamlet says, referring to his killing of Polonius, "I here proclaim was madness./ Was't Hamlet wronged Laertes? Never Hamlet/ . . . His madness was poor Hamlet's enemy." (5.2.176-86).

In the trial court, the government tried to minimize this evidence by arguing that appellant's madness was feigned, that appellant himself at one point said he intended to put "an antic disposition on." (1.5.173). But for the government to stress that one, isolated utterance is not only to overlook appellant's entire psychological profile, but also to fail to distinguish between Hamlet's feigned madness and his real madness. When Hamlet chose, as in certain obvious encounters with Polonius, Claudius, Gertrude, and others, he brilliantly pretended to be irrational. At other times, also equally obvious, appellant's genuine grief and clinical depression and delusional thinking seriously impaired his mental capacity.

SINCE LAERTES DIED WHILE ATTACKING HAMLET WITH A POISONED SWORD IN A DUEL INITIATED BY LAERTES, HAMLET ACTED IN SELF-DEFENSE

Appellant meets all the requirements of self-defense in connection with the death of Laertes. Even Laertes conceded: "I am justly killed with mine own treachery." (5.2.317).

SINCE HAMLET INNOCENTLY AND IN GOOD FAITH MISTOOK POLONIUS, WHO HID HIMSELF IN HAMLET'S MOTHER'S BEDROOM, FOR SOMEONE ELSE, POSSIBLY A MALEVOLENT INTRUDER, BURGLAR OR MURDERER, HAMLET PROPERLY INVOKED THE DEFENSE OF JUSTIFICATION

SINCE "HEART BALM" STATUTES HAVE BEEN ABOLISHED, AND SINCE OPHELIA REJECTED HAMLET FIRST, IT WOULD VIOLATE PUBLIC POLICY TO HOLD HAMLET CRIMINALLY RESPONSIBLE FOR OPHELIA'S DEATH

Presumably Ophelia committed suicide because she thought Hamlet no longer loved her. Perhaps he even broke a promise to marry her. However that may be, public policy bars fastening legal liability for her death upon Hamlet, either civilly or criminally.

Section 80-a of the New York Civil Rights Law abolishes any civil cause of action for breach of contract to marry. Although the criminal law recognizes that causing or aiding someone to commit suicide can be manslaughter (N.Y. Penal Law § 125.20) or murder (N.Y. Penal Law § 125.25), the conduct there contemplated is, to be sure, more than breaking a lover's heart, something more akin to Dr. Jack Kevorkian's much-publicized medically assisted suicides, or worse.

If male disappointment in romance is not a justification for homicide, *see, e.g. People v. Checo*, 194 A.D.2d 410, 599 N.Y.S.2d 244 (1st Dep't 1993); *People v. Hartsock*, 189 A.D.2d 991, 592 N.Y.S.2d 511 (3d Dep't 1993), neither should a female suicide resulting solely from such disappointment be a basis of criminal liability. Logic, symmetry, and feminism require no less.

Equally important is the sequence of events. Hamlet apparently lost interest in Ophelia only after Ophelia dumped him at Polonius's instructions. (1.3.90-136). Ophelia heeded her brother Laertes' warning and her father Polonius's command, and repelled Hamlet's romantic advances. (2.108-09). Polonius even went so far as to think that it was Ophelia's rejection of Hamlet that caused Hamlet's madness. (2.1.110; 2.2.96-150; 3.1.184-86). In such circumstances, to blame Hamlet for Ophelia's suicide is irrational and against the weight of the evidence.

SINCE ALL CONDUCT RELATING TO THE DEATHS OF ROSENCRANTZ AND GUILDENSTERN OCCURRED OUTSIDE DENMARK, THE TRIAL COURT HAD NO JURISDICTION TO TRY HAMLET FOR THEIR ALLEGED MURDERS

Acts charged must have been committed in this jurisdiction. N.Y. Crim. Procedure Law § 20.20. But the evidence shows that it was on a ship bound for England that Hamlet discovered that Rosencrantz and Guildenstern were escorting him there to be murdered. It was only then, aboard ship on the high seas, that Hamlet committed the acts complained of, *i.e.*, forging new documents from Claudius. On this jurisdictional ground alone, his conviction for the deaths of Rosencrantz and Guildenstern should be reversed.

SINCE HAMLET, MORE VICTIM THAN WRONGDOER, ACTED PROPERLY IN BRINGING A MURDERER TO JUSTICE, AND FOUGHT TO RESIST REVENGE, THE INDICTMENT SHOULD BE DISMISSED "IN THE INTEREST OF JUSTICE"

This peculiar case is, in more senses than one, a tragedy that cries out for dismissal "in the interest of justice." N.Y. Crim. Procedure Law § 210.40. In addition to all the obvious mitigating factors surrounding Hamlet's lack of culpability, the history, character, and condition of appellant as himself a victim of a severely dysfunctional family and a disastrous first year at law school, other compelling considerations demonstrate that appellant's conviction, a first offense, results in injustice.

Almost everyone assumes appellant had a duty to seek revenge, that he should have killed Claudius — a murderer, a regicide, and usurper on the throne — much sooner than he did. It is precisely appellant's delay in avenging his father's death that is often considered his basic weakness and that led to disaster. From this perspective, Hamlet did nothing wrong and everything right in killing Claudius. For doing so, for upholding the law, he should be praised not punished.

But this Court should also explore the thesis that Hamlet's delay does him credit as well, that appellant's indecision was an effort not to yield to the passion for revenge. Appellant's inner struggle then becomes an effort to transcend the lower morality of his time and environment and move beyond a rule of force and private vengeance to a modern rule of law. Appellant represents humanity's effort, faced with forces that would drag it backward, to ascend to a higher level. Hamlet reflects this civilizing function of law by struggling to resist the primitive call for revenge.

SINCE APPELLANT IS KING OF DENMARK, SOVEREIGN IMMUNITY REQUIRES REVERSAL ON ALL COUNTS

As the sole survivor of the royal family, Hamlet is the Danish monarch (1.2.108-09) and is therefore protected from criminal prosecutions by the doctrine of sovereign immunity. "The King can do no wrong."

When Goneril, daughter of King Lear, was asked if she admits having committed treason, her response was: "Say if I do, the laws are mine, not thine. /Who can arraign me for't?" *King Lear*, 5.3.149-50. In an era of the divine right of kings, Hamlet, an absolute monarch, is "the deputy elected by the Lord." Richard II, 3.2.53. "What subject can give sentence on his King?" *Id.*, 4.1.108. At the least, the criminal case against King Hamlet should have been stayed as long as he is in office. *See* Def.'s Brief in *Jones v. Clinton*, 520 U.S. 681 (1997).

CONCLUSION

Appellant himself should have the final say on his own appeal. After four long centuries without an appeal, appellant was right to complain bitterly of "the law's delay." (3.1.72). After reviewing the prosecutor's sophistry, we respond, as appellant did to Polonius: "Words. Words. Words." (2.2.194). And, having exposed the "rotten" State's case, we ask of the State's counsel, as did appellant of another lawyer on another occasion: "Where be his quiddits now, his quillets, his cases, his tenures, and his tricks?" (5.1.96-7).

For the reasons given, the conviction below should be reversed.

Daniel J. Kornstein

ROYAL DANISH COURT OF APPEALS
FOR THE ELSINORE CIRCUIT
_____ X

HAMLET a/k/a "The Terrorist   :
Formerly Known As Prince,"   :

                :

       Appellant   :

                :

         v.   :

                :

STATE OF DENMARK,   :

                :

       Appellee   :
_____ X

BRIEF OF APPELLEE STATE OF DENMARK*

Appellant's brief tries mightily to make an abused hero out of a ruthless monster, but it fails. Filled with "words, words, words," (2.2.207), and "quiddities" and "quillets," (5.1.91), it needs "[m]ore matter, with less art." (2.2.102).

Appellant Hamlet, a/k/a "The Terrorist Formerly Known as Prince," is a vicious serial killer, a one-man weapon of mass destruction, responsible for six "casual slaughters." (5.2.396). He hates freedom and the Danish way of life. A treasonous threat to our national security, he masterminded a shadowy international terrorist conspiracy to topple our democratically elected government, to destroy the spirit and morale of our people, to make our state "disjoint and out of frame," (1.2.20), and to grab power for himself. He almost succeeded.

In a brief but bloody spree, he assassinated our elected head of state (Claudius), murdered our prime minister (Polonius) and his two children (Ophelia and Laertes), and engineered the violent deaths of two of our diplomats (Rosencrantz and Guildenstern). Appellant even bragged of his guilt. "I could accuse me of such things," he boasted, "that it were better my mother had not borne me." (3.1.129-31). More than once he confessed to being "cruel," (3.2.394, 3.4.195), and a "rogue," (2.2.536), whose "thoughts be bloody." (3.8.69).

---

*   Submitted for a moot court in 2002 at Yale Law School.

36

For his heinous crimes, however, appellant received a "just and open trial," *The Winter's Tale*, 2.3.242, which was more than he deserved. As a terrorist who renounced his Danish citizenship, appellant could have been tried by a secret military tribunal under less strict rules of evidence and special procedures less favorable to the defense. *Presidential Order On Detention, Treatment and Trial of Certain Non-Citizens in the War Against Terrorism*, 66 Fed. Reg. 57833 (Nov. 13, 2001). [Since this was written in 2002, the Supreme Court and Congress have limited the procedures that can be utilized by such military commissions.]

I

APPELLANT, AN ENEMY COMBATANT, MAY BE DETAINED INDEFINITELY

Appellant's whining about his long imprisonment should fall on deaf ears. His claims about pre-trial detention and speedy trial dissolve because he has been detained *after* trial. Long ago appellant had his day in court, and was sentenced to life in prison. Since then, Hamlet has been inundating the courts with baseless petitions and appeals.

Appellant, a quisling and fifth column of an invasion from Norway led by Fortinbras, was an "enemy combatant." We now know, through "lawful espials," (3.1.36), approved by our top secret Foreign Intelligence Surveillance Court, that appellant, in league with Fortinbras, established and trained a secret terrorist army in Wittenberg, Germany, while pretending to go to school there. From his lair in Wittenberg, he plotted and sent his classmate and convicted co-conspirator Horatio back to Denmark to become a terrorist sleeper cell waiting for appellant's signal to spring into action.

The elected leader and commander-in-chief of Denmark has inherent power to *indefinitely* detain, without any charges, any person whom the Government designates as an "enemy combatant." Thus the Government was well within its rights in detaining appellant forever, a decision not even subject to review by this or any other court. (The Government also had the right to hold appellant incommunicado and deny him counsel, but did not do so.) [Later Supreme Court cases allowed detained "enemy combatants" to use habeas corpus to challenge their confinement.]

Life imprisonment here is neither cruel nor unusual. Many literary characters have been treated similarly or worse. Dante's *Inferno* is filled with characters condemned for eternity to imprisonment in hell. Likewise, Satan and his fellow fallen angels were, in *Paradise Lost*, also sentenced to confinement in hell forever. Greek mythology supplies many other examples: Prometheus forever chained to a rock, having his liver devoured daily by an eagle, Sisyphus forever rolling his stone uphill, etc., etc. In light of these many notable examples, appellant's far milder and shorter punishment is, *a fortiori*, neither cruel nor unusual. A contrary result would open the floodgates to countless habeas petitions from hell.

II

ANY PRETRIAL PUBLICITY WAS CAUSED BY APPELLANT AND WAS LARGELY FAVORABLE

Appellant himself was responsible for any publicity surrounding his terrorist activities. Appellant has always sought the limelight and wanted to be center stage. "Tell my story," he ordered Horatio, (5.2.358), and tell it with spin: "Report me and my cause aright." (5.2.346). Appellant, a savvy would-be politician much concerned with public opinion and media strategy, realized he had to create a new image to repair his "wounded name." (5.2.353). It was a self-inflicted wound.

Becoming appellant's first publicist, Horatio accepted his assignment with gusto: "Let me speak to the yet unknowing world how these things came about." (5.2.393-94). Horatio then carried out his task energetically, organizing an on-going multi-media disinformation campaign to burnish appellant's reputation. For a huge sum, appellant sold the magazine, book, movie, theatrical, radio, and electronic rights to his life story to one Will Shakespeare; was a consultant to all productions; and in general orchestrated a massive propaganda effort having little to do with the truth. Families of appellant's victims have sued under the Son of Sam law to obtain the money that appellant has received. 18 U.S.C. § 3681; N.Y. Exec. Law § 632-a.

Throughout his brief, appellant's counsel quotes the notoriously unreliable spin doctor Shakespeare. As the highest court in the land has ruled: "Though Shakespeare, of course/Knew the Law of his time/He was foremost a poet/In search of a rhyme." *Browning-Ferris Industries v. Kelco Disposal*, 492 U.S. 257, 285 n.7 (1989). This same Shakespeare has, for example, been much criticized for straying far from the historical truth in his docudrama about England's Richard III. "What a tribute this to art; what a misfortune this to history." Paul Kendall, *Richard the Third* 434 (1955).

That effort succeeded. Rather than the psychopathic, savage, murderous terrorist he was, appellant has been almost always portrayed favorably and sympathetically — as a thoughtful, perhaps somewhat indecisive and sad young man from a dysfunctional family, who, after much deliberation, acted correctly. The result is that today nearly everyone mistakenly thinks it was appellant's duty to kill. Appellant now exists in the public mind as a great hero in Western civilization, an idealist with exquisite moral sensibility, a charismatic intellectual. Such publicity is hardly prejudicial.

III

APPELLANT WAS PUTTING ON A "CRAZY ACT"

Appellant's "madness is surely the most interesting and challenging" aspect of this case. K.R. Eissler, *Discourse on Hamlet and HAMLET* 400 (1971). Several experts testified below on this issue for both sides. But "Hamlet's state of mind is one of those questions upon which the doctors have disagreed." Harry Levin, *The Question of Hamlet* 111 (1959).

Faced with this conflicting medical opinion, the jury concluded, as was its right, that Hamlet was not temporarily insane. This conclusion was not clearly erroneous.

Appellant admitted he was feigning insanity. Early on, appellant told his co-conspirator: "I perchance hereafter shall think meet to put an antic disposition on." (1.5.189-90). And the record runs over with proof of Hamlet's faked madness, of his "crazy act."

Only a few moments after killing Polonius, appellant himself admitted to his mother that he was not mad. "It is not madness/That I have uttered. Bring me to the test, And I the matter will reword which madness/Would gambol from." (3.4.158-61). And right after that, appellant warned his mother against letting Claudius know, "That I essentially am not in madness, But mad in craft." (3.4.205-06).

Appellant was absolutely lucid immediately before, during, and immediately after he murdered the prime minister. His conversation with the queen at that time shows him at his most rational, most insightful, and most brilliant. Appellant knew he was killing someone, and knew it was wrong. "I took thee for thy better," he exclaimed at the time. (3.4.37). He wanted to kill Claudius, but murdered Polonius instead. And then he calmly declared: "I'll lug the guts" to another room in the castle. (3.4.231). This is not madness, but clear-headed coolness under great stress.

Appellant also devised a brilliant and rational strategy to "catch the conscience of the king," (2.2.593), with evidence of his demeanor during *The Murder of Gonzago*. The jury could well have found that a man who could devise this plan and would not act on the Ghost's directive until he could ascertain its authenticity ("I'll have grounds/More relative than this") (2.2.591-92), knew that murder is wrong.

Appellant's misuse of the insanity defense closely resembles a similar ploy by former New York mob boss Vincent "Chin" Gigante, who pretended to wander aimlessly around Greenwich Village in his bathrobe in an apparent daze. The court rejected Gigante's claim of mental incompetence, calling it a "crazy act." *United States v. Gigante*, 925 F. Supp. 967, 976 (E.D.N.Y. 1996). "Defendant has been consistently feigning insanity for many years and still is doing so in a shrewd attempt to avoid punishment for his crimes." *United States v. Gigante*, 996 F. Supp. 194, 200 (E.D.N.Y. 1998). The court noted the sharp differences between the alleged insanity and Gigante's capable actions and reactions at other times, including his long history of antisocial behavior. Id. at 199. Exactly so here.

IV

CORPUS DELICTI WAS PROVEN FOR THE MURDERS OF ROSENCRANTZ AND GILDENSTERN

Appellant incorrectly argues that he cannot be convicted of murdering Rosencrantz and Guildenstern without their corpses being produced. The infamous Charles Manson, one of whose many victims was never found, made the same shopworn argument. Rejecting it, the court restated the universal rule that, "Production of the body in not a condition precedent for the prosecution for murder." *People v. Manson*, 71 Cal.App.3d 1, 42, 139 Cal.Rptr. 275, 298 (1977). Similarly, in May 2000 mother-and-son grifters Sante and Kenneth Kimes were convicted in a much-publicized

New York case of murdering an 82-year-old woman whose body was never found.

The circumstantial evidence surrounding the unexpected permanent departure of Rosencrantz and Guildenstern, highly suspicious given their personal habits and relationships, suffices to establish the corpus delicti of murder. The two victims took a short trip to England on official business. They left behind homes, substantial wealth, numerous close and powerful friends, and such personal items as dentures and eyeglasses. The missing diplomats have never again contacted their friends or relatives. These facts create a reasonable inference that the victims are dead and their death was the result of "foul and most unnatural murder." (1.5.29).

Then we have the direct eyewitness testimony, not hearsay, of the ambassador from England, where the murders occurred. Seeking thanks from Denmark, he testified that appellant's execution order was "fulfill'd" and that "Rosencrantz and Guildenstern are dead." (5.2.383-84). Appellant erroneously relies on a dramatic work by one Tom Stoppard (*Rosencrantz and Guildenstern Are Dead*) to try to show that the two victims are still alive. Not only does this argument contradict the title of the Stoppard play, but it also ignores what happens in it. At the end of Act III, Rosencrantz and Guildenstern are, in fact, dead. They vanish forever and, once again, the ambassador assures us that they are no longer with us. Besides, the Stoppard play is fiction; this case deals with fact.

Once the government presented prima facie evidence of the corpus delicti, it could then introduce appellant's confession. Appellant admitted to Horatio that he had clandestinely rewritten the message carried by Rosencrantz and Guildenstern in a diplomatic pouch so as to call for their execution. (5.2.41-50). That admission, coupled with everything else, more than satisfies the corpus delicti rule.

V

SINCE APPELLANT CAUSED OPHELIA TO COMMIT SUICIDE, HE WAS PROPERLY CONVICTED OF MURDER

Appellant, as part of his terrorist plot, planned to harm his hated political enemies by destroying the Danish prime minister's innocent and emotionally fragile young daughter. Appellant intended to drive

Ophelia to kill herself by first seducing her and making her pregnant, then abandoning her and viciously abusing and humiliating her in public. Appellant told Polonius: "Conception is a blessing, but not as your daughter may conceive, friend, look to 't." (2.2.700-701). And later Ophelia, when upset by appellant's behavior, sang: "Let in the maid that out a maid/Never departed more . . . before you tumbled me, You promised me to wed." (4.1.55-56, 63-64).

Based on this evidence, the jury properly convicted appellant of murder under Conn. Gen. Stat. § 53a-54a: "A person shall be guilty of murder when, with intent to cause death of another person, he causes the death of such person or of a third person or causes a suicide by force, duress or deception. . . ." This is not a mere civil action for "heartbreak," as appellant wishfully misdescribes it, but a criminal prosecution for intentional and premeditated homicide.

Knowing exactly how Ophelia would react, Hamlet cruelly dumped her and caused her death. Appellant's emotional battering of Ophelia makes him just as guilty of murder as if he gave her a loaded gun and told her, in her distraught state of mind, to kill herself. *Persampieri v. Commonwealth*, 343 Mass. 19, 175 N.E. 2d 387 (1961) (husband guilty of murder where he told his wife he was getting a divorce, and in response to her threat to commit suicide, taunted her and told her to get a gun and do it); *People v. Duffy*, 79 N.Y.2d 611, 584 N.Y.S.2d 739 (1972).

Ophelia's death was no accident. As a direct consequence of appellant's wrongful conduct, she "drowned herself," (5.1.5), and was for that reason denied full burial rites.

Appellant purposely pushed Ophelia over the brink. He pretended to love her, and she — gently trusting and inexperienced — believed him. After breaking all promises to her, he treated her savagely and ruthlessly. In public, before friends and family, he shamed her by acting as if he despised her and by taunting her. He called her a whore. "Nunnery was Elizabethan slang for house of prostitution." *United States v. Watson*, 423 U.S. 411, 438 n. 3 (1976) (Marshall, J., dissenting). He belittled her with disgusting and insulting gross language. He knew the unbearable pressure she was under, knew she was depressed and suicidal, knew her mind was on the verge of snapping. He knew she would kill herself, and he meant her to do so. *See* Harold Bloom, *Shakespeare* 429 (1998).

This is not only uncharitable and ungallant behavior; it is murder. "All's fair in love and war" may be the credo of a misogynist terrorist, but it is unacceptable as a rule of law or of human relations.

VI

SINCE LAERTES WAS NOT CRIMINALLY CHARGED AND APPELLANT CANNOT INVOKE SELF-DEFENSE, HIS CONVICTION FOR LAERTES' DEATH SHOULD BE AFFIRMED

Appellant cannot rely on the felony murder rule because Laertes — the victim — was never charged with a crime, let alone a felony. Nor was the felony murder rule ever intended to impose criminal liability for the intentional act of the intended victim — *i.e.*, appellant — of the original felony. *People v. Washington*, 62 Cal. 2d 777, 781 (1965).

Self-defense is likewise unavailable. The law of self-defense required appellant to retreat. His back was *not* against the wall. He could have withdrawn from the fencing match. Instead, after being wounded, appellant, "incensed," invited Laertes to "come again" and fatally wounded him. (5.2.306-07).

VII

APPELLANT IS NOT ABOVE THE LAW

After his deadly terrorist attacks, after his attempted violent overthrow of the government, after his six psychopathic murders, appellant now claims — as did Roskolnikov in *Crime and Punishment* — to be above the law. To avoid the consequences of his monstrous behavior, he tries to wrap himself in the protective doctrines of divine right of kings and sovereign immunity. It is a poor fit.

Neither doctrine applies because appellant never became king. The Danish king is elected, and appellant chose *not* to run in the election. While Claudius was campaigning for the monarchy, appellant avoided the hurlyburly of politics, refused to be a candidate, and stayed instead in Wittenberg plotting mayhem and destruction. Having never been on the ballot — butterfly or otherwise — appellant misplaces his reliance on *Bush v. Gore*, 531 U.S. 98 (2000). That case, moreover, strongly militates against interfering with the declared results of an election.

Appellant conspicuously fails to mention that after his terrorist rampage, but before his criminal trial, he was impeached (and convicted), thereby losing whatever public offices he had (including "prince"). This omission is particularly surprising inasmuch as appellant was represented throughout the impeachment proceedings by his able current counsel [David Kendall, who was Bill Clinton's lawyer], who also happens to be the most experienced impeachment defense lawyer in Denmark. Following a damning report from the court-appointed independent counsel, the Danish House of Representatives voted articles of impeachment, which led to appellant's trial and conviction in the Senate. Whatever may be the outer limits of "high crimes and misdemeanors," that phrase includes treason and murdering the king and prime minister.

Any argument based on the divine right of kings also runs up against the Constitution. The First Amendment bans the establishment of religion. And Article I of the Constitution prohibits "Titles of Nobility," which serves as a bulwark against "hereditary aristocracy and monarchy." *Federalist No. 39.*

But the real reason for rejecting appellant's attempt to avoid punishment is that no one is above the law. *United States v. Nixon,* 418 U.S. 683 (1974); *Clinton v. Jones,* 520 U.S. 681 (1997). Although *Nixon v. Fitzgerald,* 457 U.S. 731 (1982), established immunity in civil cases for official acts, this is a criminal case involving non-official acts.

CONCLUSION

Appellant's actions as well as his legal arguments put him in the malodorous and sinister company of mob boss "Chin" Gigante, mass murderer Charles Manson, and literary murderer Roskolnikov. There he belongs.

Enough quiddities and quillets! Appellant and his gang of terrorists are what is "rotten" in Denmark. "Where th' offense is/ let the great axe fall." (4.2.231).

These are perilous times. Anti-Denmarkism is rampant. Terrorism worries our people. When the law catches a violent terrorist and proves that he murdered six people, including the nation's king and prime minister, "we must not make a scarecrow of the law." *Measure for Measure,* 2.1.1. It is important to deter others. "Those many had not dared to do that evil/If the first that did th'edict infringe/Had answered for his deed." *Id.* 2.2.115-16.

For the reasons given, appellant's convictions should be affirmed. If that happens, "this business is well ended." (2.2.91). If not, then "foul deeds will rise." (1.2.279).

ROYAL DANISH COURT OF APPEALS
FOR THE ELSINORE CIRCUIT

_____ X

STATE OF DENMARK,   :

           Appellee,   :

          - against -   :

HAMLET, PRINCE OF DENMARK,   :

           Appellant.   :

_____ X

REPLY BRIEF FOR APPELLANT HAMLET

The government's brief is full of legalistic "quiddits" (*i.e.*, subtleties) and "quillets" (*i.e.*, evasions). (5.1.96-7). It has the novel, odd and revisionist distinction of quickly dispatching one of the greatest heroes in Western civilization, a most thoughtful figure, an "idealist" with exquisite "moral" sensibility, A.C. Bradley, *Shakespearean Tragedy* 111-13 (Penguin 1991) (1904), as no more than a remorseless, psychopathic "serial killer." The government's brief equates appellant with Ted Bundy. But the equation is false, the government's quillets easily exposed, and a sinister abuse of legal process unmasked.

Quillet No. 1: Although the government scoffs at appellant's argument based on lack of mental capacity, Hamlet's "madness is surely the most interesting and most challenging" aspect of this case, as one expert testified. K.R. Eissler, *Discourse on Hamlet and HAMLET* 400 (1971). But expert testimony can be found to support either side of the question. An expert cited by the government has testified, "Hamlet's state of mind is one of those questions upon which all of the doctors have disagreed." Harry Levin, *The Question of Hamlet* 111 (1959).

The record itself, rather than the divided experts' testimony, is a better guide. While stressing appellant's sometimes pretended madness, the government turns a blind eye to all proof of Hamlet's genuine emotional disturbance. The evidence will simply not support a finding that appellant was *always* faking his unbalanced mental state. Nor does it help the government to imply that talking ghosts, like UFOs, are real if seen by more than one person. The government ignores the dual character of appellant's madness, one part feigned, one part real.

What the government sarcastically dubs the "Abused Prince Syndrome" was a mental condition no different from the battered-wife syndrome, post-traumatic stress disorder or the child-abuse accommodation syndrome in that, in conjunction with mental illness, it gave rise to terrible acts of violence for which Hamlet was not responsible.

Quillet No. 2: As to Laertes' death, the government here slides over the crucial facts. Laertes conspired with Claudius to challenge Hamlet to a fencing match in which Laertes would use a poisoned sword to kill Hamlet even with a slight scratch, and then Laertes carried out those murderous plans. (4.7.108-63). Contrary to the sly innuendoes of the government's brief, Hamlet wounded Laertes with the poisoned sword *before* Laertes told him it was poisoned, and *before* Laertes confessed and implicated Claudius. (5.2.324-31). This was, after all, an athletic contest, a fencing match in which the fencers are not supposed to retreat but to attack, and in which injuries are expected to occur. The law did not require appellant to retreat in these circumstances, especially since he did not know the sword he held was tipped with poison. And since he did not know of the poisoned tip, he lacked *mens rea* and cannot be charged with the consequences of that poison.

Quillet No. 3: The government wrongly mocks appellant's defense of justification regarding Polonius's death. In addition to the justifiable use of force in the circumstances, to be found — as Polonius was — in a queen's bedroom has long been regarded as the capital crime of treason. *See* Thomas Mallory, *Le Morte d'Arthur* (1485).

Quillet No. 4: The government's fine-spun attempt to hold Hamlet criminally liable for Ophelia's death is without support in fact or law. The government misstates the record by baldly asserting that Ophelia did not reject Hamlet first. The facts are otherwise. *Before* Hamlet ever said anything unpleasant to Ophelia, she obeyed her father and brother, and "did repel" Hamlet's "letters and denied/His access to me." (2.2.108-10). The comments relied on by the government occurred *after* Ophelia, whatever her inner feelings, outwardly rejected Hamlet. The law cannot expect Hamlet to divine Ophelia's interior thoughts and feelings if they are at odds with her behavior.

On the law, the government's position is equally untenable. Lovers will have occasional quarrels, say things in the heat of the moment, and will even break up. It would violate public policy — rooted in common sense and human experience — to impose criminal liability on one lover for the emotional consequences of breaking up with the other lover. A failed romance is one of life's risks, otherwise relationships would be held hostage to threats of suicide.

Quillet No. 5: There is no evidence in the record that the "bark" transporting Hamlet and his false friends Rosencrantz and Guildenstern to England was a Danish vessel, as the government asserts. (4.3.42-48). The vessel could as easily have been an English one making a return trip, or for that matter a ship flying a Dutch or French flag. Thus, the government has failed to carry its burden of proof on the issue of jurisdiction here.

Quillet No. 6: The government's opposition to dismissal "in the interest of justice" should shock the Court's conscience. As one expert testified, "Nearly all readers, commentators, and critics are agreed in thinking that it was Hamlet's duty to kill." 1 Harold Goddard, *The Meaning of Shakespeare* 333 (1951). Indeed, two of the government's own experts — A.C. Bradley and John Dover Wilson — testified that Hamlet had such a "sacred duty." It is paradoxical to punish someone for carrying out what "nearly all" think was a sacred duty.

Quillet No. 7: In arguing against sovereign immunity for Prince (soon-to-be King) Hamlet, the government, run by Fortinbras's foreign cronies, not surprisingly misunderstands the Danish constitution. Denmark is no elective monarchy; Hamlet is its rightful King. Claudius publicly declared Hamlet to be his royal heir: "[T]hink of us/As a father: for let the world take note, /you are the most immediate to our throne." (1.2.108-09). And Rosencrantz told Hamlet, "[Y]ou have the voice of the king himself for your succession in Denmark." (3.2.354-55). Polonius also views Hamlet as Claudius's successor. (1.3.20-24).

Fortinbras is not the real king of Denmark. When he mistakenly thought he was dying, Hamlet said Fortinbras, in the power vacuum, would be king. (5.2.367-70). But Hamlet lives and he, not the foreign invader Fortinbras, is the true Danish sovereign. Fortinbras has conceded Hamlet's claim to the Danish throne, admitting that Hamlet, if he lived, would "have proved most royally." (5.2. 370, 407-09). And so he shall.

CONCLUSION

The government's argument against sovereign immunity unwittingly reveals the sinister motive behind this prosecution. It is a common story of the corrupting influence of power. Fortinbras, having seized the throne in Denmark without any lawful claim, now refuses to step down. His attorney general seeks to keep Prince Hamlet, Fortinbras's only rival, in prison for life because Hamlet is "loved" by the "multitude" (4.3.4; 4.7.18) and poses a genuine threat to Fortinbras's naked power grab. *Cf.* Richard III and the Princes in the Tower; Elizabeth I and Mary Queen of Scots.

We appeal to the integrity and the independence of this Court not to be cowed by the trappings of authority as represented by the illegal Fortinbras regime, but to do the right thing. *Cf. United States v. Nixon*, 418 U.S. 683 (1974); *N.Y. Times Co. v. United States*, 403 U.S. 713 (1971).

For the reasons given, the conviction below should be reversed.

CHAPTER 3

―――

Shylock v. Antonio

SPECIAL COURT OF APPEALS
_____ X

SHYLOCK,   :

               Appellant,   :

              -against-   :

ANTONIO,   :

               Appellee.   :
_____ X

BRIEF FOR APPELLANT SHYLOCK[*]

Prejudice is never pretty, particularly when it infects a legal proceeding. Yet such ugly prejudice — in the form of virulent anti-Semitism — irreparably marred the trial below. The facts in this simple breach of contract case are undisputed. Appellant Shylock loaned money to appellee Antonio, a wealthy importer, who failed to repay on time. Shylock sued to enforce a written loan agreement. Their contract stated

―――

[*]   Submitted for moot courts at Hofstra Law School (1996) and the New York City Bar Association (1997).

that if the borrower missed his payment, then the lender was entitled to a penalty.

At least it was a simple contract case until the biased impostor of a trial judge complicated matters unnecessarily and, in a fit of raw judicial activism, decided in Antonio's favor. The trial court in effect declared the penalty clause void against public policy, which by itself was unremarkable. But then the lower court went on to nullify the entire contract, subvert stability and certainty in commercial transactions, and, relying on an unconstitutional law, impose cruel and unusual punishments on appellant, who had merely kept his part of the bargain.

Invoking the notorious Alien Statute, the trial judge awarded half of appellant's assets to the State and half to Antonio, who said he would only "use" his half as long as Shylock lived. But, on Shylock's death, all Shylock owned had to pass to appellant's estranged daughter. The trial judge, at Antonio's specific request, also compelled appellant, a Jew, to convert to Christianity or die. (4.1.359-405).

No wonder appellant, in understandable disbelief, asked, "Is that the law?" (4.1.311). Now this Court has the chance to tell him and the rest of the world: It is not.

I

SINCE ANTI-SEMITISM TAINTED THE TRIAL, THE LOWER COURT DECISION VIOLATED THE EQUAL PROTECTION CLAUSE

Rampant anti-Semitism marred the trial below. The community in general, the witnesses, and even the trial judge were all blinded by religious prejudice. The judge herself more than once referred to appellant not by name but by the epithet "Jew." This prejudice is indisputable. *See, e.g.,* James Shapiro, *Shakespeare and the Jews* (1996); John Gross, *Shylock* (1993); Harold Bloom, "Operation Roth," *N.Y. Rev. of Books* (Apr. 22, 1993) 45, 48 ("an anti-Semitic masterpiece, unmatched in its kind"). Amid such deep and widespread prejudice, appellant could not and did not get a fair trial. *See Moore v. Dempsey*, 261 U.S. 86 (1923) (reversal where legal proceeding is a "mask" and judge is swept away by "an irresistible wave of public passion").

The general pall of thick prejudice became specific when the trial court relied on an outrageous and obviously unconstitutional law, the Alien Statute. That statute provides, in pertinent part:

> If it be prov'd against an alien
> That by direct or indirect attempts
> He seek the life of any citizen,
> The party 'against the which he doth contrive
> Shall seize one half his goods; the other half
> Comes to the privy coffer of the state;
> And the offender's life lies in the mercy
> Of the duke only, 'against all other voice.
> (4.1.360-67)

The Alien Statute, on its face and as applied, unlawfully discriminates against appellant by deeming him an alien by virtue of his religion and by treating him differently for that impermissible reason.

By singling out aliens for such treatment, and by using appellant's religion as a badge of alienage, the Alien Statute denies equal protection of the laws. *See Romer v. Evans*, 517 U.S 620 (1996) (voiding, on equal protection grounds, state constitutional amendment prohibiting laws protecting homosexuals against discrimination); Peter J. Alscher, "Staging Directions for a Balanced Resolution to the Merchant of Venice Trial Scene," 5 *Cardozo Studies in Law & Literature* 1 (1993). The statute is subject to strict scrutiny and cannot be justified by any possible governmental interest, much less a compelling one. It raises "the inevitable inference that the disadvantage imposed is born of animosity toward the class of persons affected," which "cannot constitute a *legitimate* governmental interest." *Romer, supra*, at 634, *quoting Dep't of Agriculture v. Moreno*, 413 U.S. 528, 534 (1973).

By virtue of this law, a Jew does not have the same rights as a citizen of Venice. It constitutes unequal treatment by the State, takes away the civil rights of Jews, and deprives Jews of the rights to private property. The obnoxious Alien Statute thus joins the Nuremburg laws, Jim Crow laws, and South African apartheid laws as repugnant to basic notions of decency.

II

SINCE THE TRIAL "JUDGE" WAS MARRIED TO ANTONIO'S BEST FRIEND (FOR WHOM THE LOAN WAS MADE) AND WAS NEITHER A LAWYER NOR A JUDGE, SHE WAS BIASED AND INCOMPETENT

Appellant was entitled to an impartial judge, and Portia was neither impartial nor a judge. A party is deprived of due process of law when his or her liberty or property is subject to the decision of a judge who has a personal or pecuniary interest in the outcome. *Tumey v. Ohio*, 273 U.S. 510 (1927). Portia violated Canon 2B of the *Code of Judicial Conduct* by allowing her "family, social or other relationships to influence" her judicial conduct or judgment. She should have recused herself under Canon 3 C(l)(a) of the *Code of Judicial Conduct*, because her impartiality "might reasonably be questioned" inasmuch as she "has a personal bias or prejudice concerning a party, or personal knowledge of disputed evidentiary facts concerning the proceedings."

And of course Portia committed a crime by impersonating a judge and practicing law without a license. N.Y. Judiciary Law § 478 (unlawful practice of law); § 484 (same); § 492 (use of attorney's name— Balthasar—by Portia).

III

SINCE APPELLANT WAS ORDERED IN A CIVIL CASE TO PAY OVER ALL HIS PROPERTY AND CONVERT TO ANOTHER RELIGION, THE JUDGMENT BELOW CONSTITUTED CRUEL AND UNUSUAL PUNISHMENT AND VIOLATED DUE PROCESS

Appellant's civil suit on a loan agreement should never have ended up in severe criminal penalties against him. He received no prior notice of any criminal charges. The trial judge trotted out the criminal statute for the first time in the middle of the trial. This alone violates due process.

By any measure, the severe penalties actually imposed on appellant constitute cruel and unusual punishment. They degrade the dignity of humans beings, they are arbitrary, they are unacceptable to contemporary society, and they are excessive. *See Furman v. Georgia*, 408 U.S. 238, 270-82 (1972) (Brennan, J. concurring).

IV

SINCE THE TRIAL "JUDGE" IMPROPERLY REQUIRED PLAINTIFF TO CONVERT TO CHRISTIANITY, THE COURT VIOLATED THE FIRST AMENDMENT'S FREE EXERCISE AND ESTABLISHMENT CLAUSES

Freedom of religion means that the trial court's order to appellant that he convert to another religion is null and void. That order simultaneously violates both aspects of the Religion Clause. It abridges appellant's freedom to worship in the religion of his own choice and it "force[s] him to profess a belief" in a particular religion. *Everson v. Board of Education*, 330 U.S. 1, 15 (1947).

V

SINCE APPELLANT WAIVES SPECIFIC PERFORMANCE OF THE PENALTY CLAUSE, THE REST OF THE CONTRACT IS ENFORCEABLE AND APPELLANT IS ENTITLED TO PRINCIPAL PLUS INTEREST

Appellant no longer seeks his pound of flesh. Even during the trial, appellant stated: "Give me my principal, and let me go." (4.1.348). With that controversial issue waived and therefore out of the case, appellant is entitled to principal and interest.

The whole controversy over the equitable remedy of specific performance of the penalty clause could have been easily avoided. All the trial judge had to do was find that Shylock had an adequate remedy at law for damages (*i.e.*, principal and interest) and award those damages, while denying specific performance. In not doing so, the court below erred by failing to enforce the contract, thereby jeopardizing stability and certainty in commercial law, a point conceded by both Antonio and Portia. (3.126-31; 4.1.215-19).

To deny appellant principal and interest would, moreover, give appellee a tremendous windfall. Three of his ships did return safely, after the trial, with huge profit to Antonio. (5.1.295-96). In such circumstances, it would be unjust in the extreme to deny appellant recovery. The safe return of Antonio's three ships supplies a basis for mutual mistake — everyone was under the misimpression that they were lost. Now Antonio can pay the debt.

CONCLUSION

Appellant was victimized and degraded in the trial court. The decision below, as many have noted, embodies raw anti-Semitism and encourages persecution against Jews. This Court, however, should assert itself and strike a blow for freedom of religion, liberty of contract, and equal protection of the laws.

At one point during the proceedings, Shylock movingly asked: "Hath not a Jew eyes?" (3.1.52). On behalf of him and all other minority members, we now ask this Court: Hath not a Jew (or any other minority member) rights?

For the reasons given, the Alien Statute should be declared unconstitutional, the judgment below should be reversed, appellant should be awarded principal plus interest, and the Court should make a criminal reference to the attorney general about Portia impersonating a judge and practicing law without a license. N.Y. Judiciary Law § 476-a.

As appellant rightly exclaimed below: "If you deny me, fie upon your law!" (4. 1.100).

SPECIAL COURT OF APPEALS
_____ X

SHYLOCK,   :

        Appellant,   :

        -against-   :

ANTONIO,   :

        Appellee.   :
_____ X

BRIEF FOR APPELLEE ANTONIO*

Few issues could be more basic or more timely than those presented by this case. At stake are not only competing considerations of legal doctrine and public policy, but a man's life. To enforce a "strange" loan agreement (4.1.180), appellant Shylock invokes freedom of contract and stability and certainty in commercial law, especially here in Venice, New York, commercial and financial center of the world. Appellee Antonio insists that public policy limits freedom of contract, and that some contracts are illegal and, as a matter of public policy, should not be enforced. Which view should prevail today, on the facts of this case and in the midst of a worldwide economic bloodletting, will determine the outcome of this appeal.

A Tainted CDO. This case is about a collateralized debt obligation (CDO) so obviously illegal on its face that it is void and unenforceable in all respects. This tainted CDO — the quintessentially toxic loan agreement — specifies the mortgage collateral as an unmonetizable pound of flesh nearest Antonio's heart and contains a penalty clause that by its plain meaning (and as sought to be enforced by Shylock) requires Antonio to die for not repaying the loan on time. (Antonio could not repay the loan on time because of an economic meltdown. News of his ships being lost plus a worldwide collapse of credit markets made

---

* Submitted for a 2008 moot court at Cardozo Law School in New York City.

repayment impossible.) This horrific penalty clause violates public policy and invalidates the whole contract.

Standard of Review. Given the issues, the parties agree that the standard of review is for this Court to examine the contract's clear and unambiguous language de novo. Insofar as the trial court (Portia, J.) dismissed Shylock's pro se complaint, that ruling should be affirmed. In certain other respects, however, the decision below should be vacated and modified.

At the outset it will help to identify what issues are and are not involved on this appeal.

ISSUES ON APPEAL

Though important and far-reaching, the issues on appeal are few and precise. The key issue is whether the loan agreement between the parties is void as against public policy because of its fatal penalty clause. The answer to that almost rhetorical question is a resounding "yes."

That affirmative answer leads in turn to the practical issues of what relief Antonio is entitled to. In the circumstances of this case, Antonio deserves a judgment declaring that the loan agreement is void, that he does not have to repay any part of the loan, that he is entitled to attorney's fees, and that Shylock should be enjoined from bringing any more suits on the loan.

ISSUES NOT ON APPEAL

Shylock tries to distract and confuse this Court by raising several unsavory red herrings (neither pickled, nor in cream sauce). Contrary to what Shylock's attorney says, this appeal is *not* about the Alien Statute, is *not* about Judge Portia's bias or fraud, is *not* about Shylock's forced religious conversion, is *not* about compelling Shylock to bequeath half of his estate to his estranged daughter, and is *not* about compelling Shylock to forfeit the rest of his estate to the State.

Issues Waived. Antonio waives all these issues, forgoes any such "lender liability" relief he won below based on them, and abandons these points. In the four hundred years that this appeal has evolved and been pending on this Court's crowded docket, Antonio has been reconstructed: he has had time for his anger and prejudice to ebb and, after further reflection (and counsel's guidance), to narrow his claims and defenses. On this appeal, Antonio is concerned only with the loan agreement and, once and for all, wiping out his obligation under that agreement.

Religious Prejudice Irrelevant. Shylock is playing the religion card, but this is not a case about religious discrimination. It is about an illegal contract. On this appeal, we neither deny nor defend the unfortunate and despicable anti-Semitism surrounding the trial. But, this being a matter of de novo contract interpretation on appeal, whether or not the trial was unfair and thereby marred by bias is irrelevant and beside the point.

The underlying core issue at trial — as on appeal — is the legality of the penalty clause. As a matter of law, this question requires no trial of disputed facts and is immune to the effects of prejudice. The written contract is — and remains — what it is, regardless of what took place below. This Court's function is to discern the meaning intended by the parties, as stated in the objective, unequivocal language of the contract. As a result, the so-called errors alleged by Shylock are harmless and irrelevant. *See, e.g., Faulkner v. Nat'l Geographic Enters., Inc.*, 409 F.3d 26, 42 n.10 (2d Cir. 2005) (failure to recuse is "at most harmless error" where, after de novo review, appellate court affirms summary judgment against appellant). The parties' contract, annexed hereto as Exhibit A, contained a choice of law clause specifying that New York and American federal law circa 2008 would govern any disputes.

I

THE CONTRACT VIOLATES PUBLIC POLICY

The starting point on this appeal is public policy. Both parties agree on the controlling legal standard but disagree on how to apply it. Both parties agree that freedom of contract has limits. We further agree with Shylock's counsel that "commercial contracts are to be enforced according to their terms unless doing so would be contrary to an overriding public policy."

But we part company over whether the contract in question actually does clash with overriding public policy. We say it does, Shylock's attorney says it does not.

A. Relevant Public Policy

To find the governing public policy, this Court can look to legislation, legal precedents, and the common attitudes of our community and our notions of what makes for the general welfare — "the felt necessities of the time, the prevalent moral and political theories, intuitions of public policy, avowed or unconscious." O.W. Holmes, *The Common Law* 1 (1881). The "void against public policy" doctrine is based more on common sense, fairness, and natural law than on technical legal concepts.

With these sources in mind, who can doubt that the penalty of the parties' loan agreement — a pound of flesh in Antonio's "breast nearest his heart" — violates overriding public policy? "No civilized . . . legal system would enforce a penalty bond of this character." Richard A. Posner, *Law and Literature* 93 (1988). "Enforcement of the bond would be absurd." *Id.* at 96. *See also id.* at 106. As a matter of public policy, courts will not enforce a contract that involves A "holding a knife at B's throat," Richard A. Posner, *Economic Analysis of Law* § 4.6 at 80 (2d ed. 1977), exactly the situation here. [Judge Posner was chief judge of the moot court.]

B. Feeble Counter-Argument

Shylock's feeble attempt at constructing an offsetting public policy argument is half-hearted at best and disingenuous at worst. The loan agreement, it is asserted by Shylock's counsel, is unusual but does not contravene Venetian public policy. This is so, we are told, because removing a pound of flesh from Antonio's body would be a mere inconvenience, comparable to a safe, minimally invasive medical procedure such as liposuction. *Id. Cf.* liposuction advertisement — "Lose up to 8 lbs. In 1 hour!" — from N.Y. Times, Nov. 13, 2008. Any hesitation or queasiness on the Court's part regarding such a penalty, argues Shylock, should yield to the countervailing and supposedly more powerful public policies behind freedom of contract, commercial stability, and anti-obesity.

Empty Lawyer-Talk. This facetious argument is pure sophistry. Shylock's counsel himself does not believe it. "It must be conceded," Shylock's lawyer grudgingly admits with his tongue in his cheek, "that reasonable minds might differ on this point." "There is something undignified," he goes on (and putting it rather mildly), "about the possibility that a Venetian court might order a Venetian citizen to mutilate his or her body to satisfy a debt." "Undignified," to say the least. How about uncivilized, inhuman, and barbaric? Simply put, the public policy against murder or mutilation overrides any policy favoring enforcement of commercial contracts.

Stubborn Facts. Shylock's less than candid attempt to trivialize the genuine threat to Antonio's life, moreover, runs up against stubborn undisputed facts. Shylock did not ask Antonio to improve his health by diet or exercise. Rather, Shylock came to trial brandishing a knife, sharpening it in the presence of the court, and demanding the pound of flesh nearest Antonio's heart. (4.1.124). From the start, Shylock's hope and intent was to use the penalty clause to kill Antonio. It is undisputed that in insisting on that provision, Shylock snarled: "I hate him [*i.e.*, Antonio]. . . . If I can catch him once upon the hip I will feed fat the ancient grudge I bear him. . . . Cursed be my tribe if I forgive him." (1.3.38-48).

C. Not Liquidated Damages

Equally unavailing is any attempt by Shylock to try to characterize the default penalty as a permissible garden variety liquidated damages clause. To pass muster, a liquidated damages provision must bear a rational economic relationship to plaintiff's loss, and attempt "to estimate the actual damages caused by the breach." Posner, *Economic Analysis of Law, supra*, § 4.10, at 93. *See also U.S. Fidelity and Guar. Co. v. Braspetro Oil Services*, 369 F.3d 34, 72-73 (2d Cir. 2004) (default clause unenforceable where not a reasonable measure of loss). No rational relationship exists here between the penalty insisted on and Shylock's loss.

CDOs, like the one here, are notoriously hard to value and are virtually worthless today. The loan was for 3000 ducats, but the collateral — a pound of Antonio's flesh — was sub-prime. Antonio, a sedentary merchant, did not follow a regular exercise program. The collateral is worth much less than 3000 ducats, as Shylock conceded at trial (a pound of Antonio's flesh is not that "estimable" or "profitable" — 1.3.167-69). It is not even a human organ, such as a heart, which might have real market value if needed for a medical transplant. It is only flesh.

D. Shylock Subverts His Own Pseudo-Economic Theory

The deadly punitive as opposed to reasonable economic nature of the default provision emerged with great clarity when Shylock refused at trial to accept two and even three times the principal. In the court below, Shylock tried unsuccessfully to hide his true intent in the guise of economic theory. It did not work.

A pound of Antonio's flesh may have negligible monetary value on an open market, but has great value to Shylock for personal reasons. That pound of flesh, claimed Shylock at trial, is "dearly bought," (4.1.101-02), implicitly referring to all the indignities and humiliations Shylock has had to suffer from anti-Semitism. Different people, Shylock testified, value things differently, and more than that he will "give no reason" and will "not answer." (4.1.41-63).

But then Shylock destroys his own argument. He concedes that ill-will and malice, not economics, motivate him. He expressly admits the "lodged hate and certain loathing I bear Antonio" as the reason for pursuing a "losing suit" and seeking an obviously uneconomic legal remedy. (4.1.61-63). With that damning admission, any possible economic prop for Shylock's liquidated damages argument evaporated.

E. Affirm on Any Ground in Record

To the extent any other portion of the decision below implies that the penalty is lawful and could be enforced, it should be vacated. More than once, the lower court seems to say that the penalty is legally enforceable so long as it is done precisely according to its terms and does not violate other laws. Ultimately, for these latter reasons, the lower court does not enforce the penalty. Although the lower court comes to the right result but by the wrong route, this Court can affirm on any ground supported by the record. *McNally Wellman Co. v. N.Y. State Elec. & Gas Corp.*, 63 F.3d 1188 (2d Cir. 1995). Thus the dismissal of Shylock's complaint can and should be upheld even if the trial judges's rationale was incorrect.

II

THE ILLEGAL CONTRACT IS VOID

Once it is determined that the loan agreement violates public policy, the next question is to decide the consequences of that determination. Those consequences are huge.

A. Void and Unenforceable

As a result of his gross violation of public policy, Shylock has, as a matter of law, forfeited his right to sue under the loan agreement either for principal or interest. "Penalties such as this are void ab initio as a matter of public policy." *Wells Fargo Northwest Bank v. Varig-S.A.*, 2003 WL 21508341 (S.D.N.Y. June 27, 2003) (Rakoff, J.). [Judge Jed Rakoff, a federal judge in Manhattan, was another judge on this moot court.] A contract based on an unlawful promise is unenforceable. 6A Arthur Corbin, *Corbin on Contracts* § 1522 (1962); 2 E. Allan Farnsworth, *Farnsworth on Contracts* § 5 (1990).

B. Analogy to Usury

This conclusion follows by analogy from the way the law treats usurious contracts. Although Shylock's ordinary practice, as the record makes clear, was to charge interest on loans, he did not do so with Antonio, inserting instead the grisly penalty clause. Thus the penalty clause here can usefully be thought of as a substitute for interest, and illegal interest at that. It is highly instructive therefore to look at the law of usury.

According to New York General Obligations Law § 5-511(2), the court "shall declare" a usurious contract "to be void, and enjoin any prosecution thereon, and order the same to be surrendered and cancelled." Usurious loans are accordingly void as a matter of law. As a result, were the transaction at issue no more than a usurious loan, "the borrower is relieved of all further payment — not only interest but also outstanding principal, and any mortgages securing payment and walk away from the agreement." *Seidel v. 18 East 17th Street Owners, Inc.* 79 N.Y.2d 735, 740, 586 N.Y.S.2d 240, 242 (1992). Though perhaps harsh, these "prescribed consequences are necessary to deter the evils of usury." *Id.*

C. The Rule Applied

This salutary rule should apply with even greater force and reason to the illegal loan agreement here. The public policy against usury is not nearly as strong as the policy against murder. The underlying concern of the law to protect desperate people from the baleful consequences of their own desperation must be vindicated in this case. If something as innocuous as usury requires a lender to forfeit principal as well as interest, then a lender who insists on a penalty clause requiring a borrower's death should a fortiori forfeit at least as much. This consequence is only common sense and is necessary to deter the evils of deadly overreaching by unscrupulous and predatory lenders.

D. Economic Analysis

The same result occurs as a matter of economic theory. Normally, performance of a contract should be encouraged because it results in a value-increasing, voluntary exchange. But that presumption is rebutted where the contract is infected with conduct society wants to discourage as a matter of public policy. Just as when the promise is induced by fraud, so too here when non-performance triggers a murderous penalty clause, "not only would enforcement not facilitate voluntary exchange, but non-enforcement may serve to discourage such conduct in the future." Posner, *Economic Analysis of Law, supra*, § 4.6.

III

THE OFFENDING CLAUSE IS NON-SEVERABLE

To avoid the consequences of his illegal penalty clause, Shylock tries to jettison it from his argument. But the invalid death penalty clause cannot be severed from the rest of the contract. The agreement itself contains no severability clause, *see* Exhibit A hereto, which might otherwise permit the rest of the agreement to be enforceable. In any event, regardless of a severability clause, the entire contract should be declared void, again as a matter of public policy. The penalty here is not incidental, but, rather, goes to the heart of the transaction — Antonio's heart. Where a contract provision is so "heinous in character," as here, the contract is "not divisible" and the illegality is such as to "taint" the whole consideration. 6A *Corbin on Contracts, supra*, § 1522 at 762 n.32.

Nor can Shylock's belated mid-trial change of heart as to remedies affect the outcome. We hear now that Shylock wants to waive specific performance and accept money damages alone, that is, repayment of principal and interest. But Shylock's tardy election of remedies is too little too late, a transparent attempt to sever the penalty clause by another means, and should be rejected. Having engineered his illegal contract, Shylock cannot now disassociate himself from it.

IV

NO EXCEPTION APPLIES

Although exceptions to the general rules governing illegal contracts exist, none of those exceptions apply here. *See Seidel, supra,* 79 N.Y.2d at 740-41, 586 N.Y.S.2d at 742-43. Antonio has standing to raise the defense. He is not a stranger to the transaction; he is both borrower and mortgagor.

Nor is Antonio estopped from asserting the defense. A special relationship of trust and confidence did not exist between Antonio and Shylock; Antonio was not Shylock's fiduciary. Quite the contrary. It is not disputed that they hated each other and did not trust each other in the least. *Compare Pemper v. Reiffer,* 264 A.D.2d 625, 695 N.Y.S.2d 555 (1st Dep't 1999) (summary judgment inappropriate where borrower, in relationship of trust and experienced in finance, proposed usurious interest rate and allegedly misled lenders about legality of transaction). Antonio, moreover, did not propose the obnoxious penalty, Shylock did. (1.3.145-53). Antonio did nothing to induce Shylock to rely on the legality of the transaction. Shylock was and is a canny, successful, and experienced money lender. He, not Antonio, intentionally had a notary prepare the agreement (1.3.146-47, 174-75); Antonio had no intention of avoiding repayment. (1.3.158). *See Pemper v. Reiffer, supra; Russo v. Carey,* 271 A.D.2d 889, 706 N.Y.S.2d 760 (3rd Dep't 2000).

And Antonio cannot be deemed to have waived the affirmative defense of illegality. It is true that at trial Antonio did not explicitly challenge the penalty clause on public policy grounds and even thought — mistakenly — that he had no defense. (4.1.10-14, 85, 249-50, 273-90). But Antonio was unrepresented; he appeared pro se and this Court should give him leeway when it comes to procedural technicalities. *In re Sims,* 534 F.2d 117, 133 (2d Cir. 2008). More importantly, a defense based on public policy can, by its very nature, never be waived. The law does not permit a private litigant to waive a defense affecting the public. This Court should therefore find no waiver, just as Judge Rakoff did in *Wells Fargo Northwest Bank v. Varig-S.A,* 2003 WL 21508341 (S.D.N.Y. June 27, 2003) at *7 (waiver of defenses clause ineffective to waive an illegal penalty).

V

ALTERNATIVE GROUNDS EXIST
FOR NON-ENFORCEMENT

Public policy regarding the heinous nature of the penalty clause is only one reason for not enforcing the loan agreement. There are two others. One is that the loan agreement also violates public policy as a gambling contract. It is not a commercial venture, but as our Chief Judge has stated elsewhere, a gamble on Antonio's life. Richard A. Posner, *Law and Literature* 93 (1988).

The other alternate ground for denying enforcement is fraud. The record supports the inference that Shylock proposed the penalty clause to Antonio as a jest. Shylock himself fraudulently induced Antonio to agree to the bond on the ground that it was only "a merry sport" (1.3.144) and not meant seriously. This was a false, material misrepresentation.

VI

ATTORNEY'S FEES

Not only should Shylock's suit be dismissed, but Antonio should recover his appellate attorney's fees on two grounds. First, this suit was frivolous, sham and without a reasonable basis in law or in fact. *See* Fed. R. Civ. P. 11; N.Y. Local Rules § 130-1.1. Second, the parties' loan agreement — the "bond" — contains a clause providing that the prevailing party in any litigation arising out of the transaction will recover reasonable attorney's fees from the other party. *See* Exhibit A hereto. Having prevailed, Antonio should be awarded attorney's fees for this reason as well.

VII

INJUNCTION

"The law hath yet another hold" on Shylock. (4.1.360). The time has come at long last to bring down the final curtain on this long-running farce. A high-profile controversy, this case has generated much public interest and commentary for four centuries. Plays, movies, and docudramas have been based on this case. Shylock has sued Antonio countless times, with the same result over and over again, and these meritless lawsuits must end.

Shylock is obsessed with this litigation almost to the point of psychosis. His behavior throughout the trial was vengeful and irrational. Driven to the brink of madness (and perhaps beyond) by his daughter's elopement and theft of his jewels, Shylock rejected three times the principal. Without judicial intervention, Shylock will never stop. This Court should enjoin appellant from bringing any further such suits without permission of this Court. *See In re Martin-Trigona*, 573 F.Supp. 1245 (D. Conn. 1983), *aff'd*, 737 F.2d 1254 (2d Cir. 1984).

CONCLUSION

To borrow an apt and heart-felt statement by Justice Felix Frankfurter, "one who belongs to the most vilified and persecuted minority in history is not likely to be insensible" to claims of anti-Semitism in a judicial proceeding. *West Virginia State Bd. of Education v. Barnette*, 319 U.S. 624, 646 (1943) (dissenting opinion). "But as judges we are neither Jew nor gentile, neither Catholic nor agnostic." *Id.*

The incontrovertible fact is that, regardless of any religious prejudice, Antonio was and is entitled to the limited relief he seeks on this appeal. To uphold Shylock's position is to invite predatory behavior by lenders, which may well have caused the current economic meltdown.

For the reasons given, the judgment should be affirmed insofar as it dismissed Shylock's lawsuit, and should be vacated and modified so that the loan agreement is declared void and unenforceable. To recover any loss in connection with his ill-conceived CDO, appellant, as a lender, may apply for a government bailout.

EXHIBIT A

NON-NEGOTIABLE PROMISSORY NOTE WITH BOND

3000 Ducats, Venetian

At the Notary, The Rialto,
Venice, New York
Made: This 10th day of the month
of April, 1595

1. LOAN AMOUNT AND TERMS OF REPAYMENT

FOR VALUE RECEIVED OF 3000 Ducats, Venetian (the "Moneys"), and for other good and sufficient consideration, the undersigned Antonio, residing at the Ca D'Oro, Canalasso ("Borrower"), promises to repay to the undersigned Shylock, residing near to the Scuola Grande Tedesca in the Ghetto of Venice ("Lender"), the aforesaid Moneys in the principal sum of 3000 Ducats, with 0% (zero percent) usance, said Moneys to be paid three months to the date set forth above as the making of this Note and said payment to be made at the Notary of Venice, The Rialto, Venice, New York, or such other place as the Lender may designate.

2. BOND

Should Borrower fail to repay the Moneys at the time due under this Note, Borrower shall forfeit his Bond, here given in security for this Note, said Bond being a pound of flesh to be cut off and taken in what part of Borrower's body pleaseth Lender, which Lender herein designates as the part of Borrower's breast nearest his heart.

3. NO ACCELERATION

The Lender has no right to accelerate the time due for repayment for any reason.

4. ATTORNEYS' FEES

If any legal action or other proceeding is brought for the enforcement of this Note, the prevailing party, in addition to any other relief to which he may be entitled, shall be entitled to recover reasonable attorneys' fees or other costs incurred in connection with such action or proceeding and in any petition for appeal or appeal therefrom.

5. <u>NOTICE</u>

Any notice to Borrower with respect to this Note shall be given by Duke's Courier, return receipt requested, addressed to Borrower at his address stated above, or to such other address as Borrower may designate by notice to Lender. Any notice to Lender shall be given by Duke's Courier, return receipt requested, addressed to the Lender at his address stated above, or at such other address as may have been designated by notice to Borrower.

6. <u>GOVERNING LAW</u>

This Note shall be governed by the laws of the State of New York and the, United States of America, circa 2008.

7. <u>CHOICE OF FORUM</u>

Any action or proceeding brought for the enforcement of or otherwise in relation to this Note shall be brought in the Courts for and within the jurisdiction of Cardozo Law School.

8. <u>ENTIRE AGREEMENT</u>

This Note constitutes the entire agreement between the Borrow and Lender and may be modified only on unanimous written consent.

_____/s/_____
Antonio, Borrower

ACCEPTED:

_____/s/_____
Shylock, Lender

WITNESSED AND SEALED:

_____/s/_____
Notary of Venice

SPECIAL COURT OF APPEALS

———————————————————— X

SHYLOCK, :

                    Appellant, :

                    -against- :

ANTONIO, :

                    Appellee. :

———————————————————— X

REPLY BRIEF FOR APPELLANT SHYLOCK

Appellee Antonio's brief offers no good reason — much less a cogent one — for affirming the intolerable decision below. On the contrary, Antonio's brief is a curious and extraordinary document, curious in what it says and extraordinary in what it does not say. Unhappy with the trial record and the applicable law, Antonio vainly tries to ignore both.

Appellee's brief is an example of what one of the trial witnesses — an early and prescient champion of litigation reform — described memorably:

> In law, what plea so tainted and corrupt
> But, being seasoned with a gracious voice,
> Obscures the show of evil. (3.2.75-79).

Indeed. This Court should cut through Antonio's sophistry, pull the mask off the pretense of a trial below, and reverse.

1. What appellee's brief fails to say catches the eye immediately. A glance at Antonio's brief shows that it says absolutely nothing in response to many of our most compelling points, and almost nothing about the rest. Such conspicuous silence is understandable, given the lack of merit in Antonio's position.

Antonio fails, for example, to rebut the indisputable evidence that the phoney trial judge was biased and incompetent. He does not

— because he cannot — even attempt to explain or justify Portia's gross misbehavior. As another court has held in a related case, the record here

> presents a disturbing picture of Portia's actions as a jurist. The record makes evident that Portia appeared in disguise because she, in fact, was not learned in the law, and that, having gained a position of power under false pretenses, proceeded to abuse that position at the trial by acting in a mean, prejudiced and vindictive manner toward Shylock.

David B. Saxe, "Shylock, Portia and a Case of Literary Oppression," 5 *Cardozo Studies in Law and Literature* 115, 118 (1993). In short, "Portia's actions at the trial were outrageous; she violated the most basic principles of fairness and impartiality." *Id.* at 121.

Equally unrebutted are appellant's other arguments. Antonio offers no equal protection analysis that would save the patently discriminatory Alien Statute. Nor does Antonio seriously deny the anti-Semitic tenor of the trial. He also fails to answer the arguments based on cruel and unusual punishment and due process violations. As for the massive violation of Shylock's First Amendment rights, Antonio has virtually nothing to say.

2. Antonio's appellate silence on crucial points is matched by the hollowness of the little he does say on other issues. A good example is Antonio's blithe but baseless assertion that Shylock "consented" to the awful punishments imposed on him as part of a "negotiated settlement." Faced with a choice between death or lesser punishments, Shylock chose to live, but such a choice is hardly consent freely given. The law does not recognize a choice made under such circumstances of extreme threat and duress as legal consent.

But Antonio's disingenuous argument based on Shylock's compelled consent is typical. Prejudice at trial? No, says Antonio, "it was justice the court meted out." Religious bias? No, argues appellee, merely evil justly rewarded. The Alien Statute unconstitutional? No, asserts Antonio, "largely a problem of literature not law." These are not reasoned legal arguments, but glib one-liners designed to stifle serious discussion.

Even Antonio's most serious argument — lack of severability of an unconscionable contract provision — should be rejected. This Court cannot ignore the conditions out of which the loan agreement arose: the long and provocative history of religious prejudice and abuse suffered by Shylock at the hands of Antonio and his anti-Semitic friends, the spirit of jocularity in which the penalty provision was created, and the widowed Shylock's breakdown on learning that his only daughter had run away with his money to marry out of the faith. Public policy considerations, moreover, do not all point in Antonio's favor. He has obtained a huge windfall as a result of the decision below, while Shylock has lost his principal plus interest.

Antonio's effort to blame Shylock for not accepting the principal at trial will not work either. Shylock's refusal was based on Judge Portia's misleading him about his chances of winning. The trial judge raised Shylock's expectations of success so that he rebuffed settlement. (4.1.175-76, 227-30, 244-46). Now she and her wily ways have been exposed.

Even the legal precedent relied on by Antonio — *Garrity v. Lyle Stuart, Inc.*, 40 N.Y.2d 354 (1976) — has been seriously eroded. The Appellate Division specifically held that *Garrity* will not stand in the way of private parties seeking punitive damages under a contract arbitration clause. *Mulder v. Donaldson, Lufkin & Jenrette*, 224 A.D.2d 125 (1st Dep't 1996). Thus freedom of contract does allow some scope to penalty clauses.

3. At a loss for argument, Antonio retreats to the last refuge of appellate advocacy: wanting different facts and different law. But the transparent attempt to rewrite the record and import inapplicable law must fail. Antonio is so unhappy with the trial record that he urges this Court not to accept that record "too much at face value." In other words, Antonio does not like the facts, dubbing them "satire" and "fairy tale."

But the facts are true facts; what happened at the trial is what we are appealing from. Antonio cannot wish them away. Nor can Antonio wish away the applicable law. This appeal is governed by American law circa 1996. To describe such law, as Antonio does, as "the unforgivingly politically correct lens of contemporary legal and social mores" is to miss the point. This is not an appeal based on medieval Venetian law, whatever that may be. The purpose of the appeal, by stipulation of the parties and the Court, is to see how the case would be argued in today's legal climate, as if it arose in Venice, New York.

CONCLUSION

"Truth will come to light," one of the trial witnesses exclaimed, "in the end truth will out." (2.2.72-74). Only this Court can ensure that happy result. For the reasons given here and in our main brief, the decision of the court below should be reversed. We have conservatively calculated the interest (at the statutory rate of 9% simple interest annually) due since the year 1600 (that is, 411 years) on appellant's loan of 3,000 ducats to be 110,970 ducats (that is, 3000 x .09 x 411 = 110,970 ducats).

CHAPTER 4

The People's Voices
(Coriolanus)

Hamlet and *Merchant* are two of the greatest and most frequently performed of Shakespeare's plays, and for those reasons are well known. But others, less well known, also deserve attention, especially at particular times.

Around election time, for instance, there is one Shakespeare play Americans should think about more than any other, and it is *Coriolanus*. *Coriolanus* is a play about politics, running for public office, counting votes — in short, about democracy. Every politician, especially every presidential candidate, should carefully read and mull over *Coriolanus*. Its political message may explain why this play is always so relevant, always so extraordinarily timely, and always so riveting, even if it is rarely performed.

Inasmuch as politics, elections, and democracy form a large basis of our law — the radical critical legal studies movement insists that law is nothing more than politics — *Coriolanus* is a play about law, public law grandly conceived. Seeing these large themes, English critic William Hazlitt wrote in the early nineteenth century:

> Anyone who studies [*Coriolanus*] may save himself the trouble of reading Burke's *Reflections*, or Paine's *Rights of Man*, or the Debates in both Houses of Parliament since the French Revolution or our own. The arguments for and against aristocracy or democracy, on the privileges of the few and the claims of the many, on liberty and slavery, power and abuse of it, peace and war, are here very ably handled, with the spirit of a poet and the acuteness of a philosopher.

Coriolanus thus becomes a primer, in dramatic form, on constitutional law.

The large political (and therefore legal) themes in *Coriolanus* flow from the tragedy of a soldier-politician-aristocrat in ancient Rome. Caius Marcius, patrician by birth, wins military glory for Rome by decisively defeating Rome's enemies, the Volscians, at the battle of Corioli. So splendid is his prowess in battle that he is henceforth called Coriolanus, after the site of the battle, just as in World War II British Field Marshal Bernard Montgomery became known as "Montgomery of Alamein" in honor of his great victory over the Germans under Rommel at El Alamein in North Africa.

Coriolanus returns in triumph to Rome where his fellow patricians, believing they have found an unbeatable political candidate, prevail on him to run for high office. So far, nothing in *Coriolanus* is alien to American playgoers who have in their own national memory the similar examples of George Washington, Ulysses Grant, Dwight Eisenhower, and others. That tradition continues. After Operation Desert Storm in 1991, both major political parties attempted to court General Colin Powell and General Norman Schwartzkopf to be part of the 1992 ticket. A few years after that, General Wesley Clark tested the electoral waters. Making this part of the play even more keen today is the real possibility that General David Petraeus will some day run for high office. Clearly, ever since George Washington's example, military success has been a good jumping off point for a political career in America.

But, unlike today's soldier-politicians with splendid war records, Coriolanus does not want to run on his. He comes before the voters and asks:

> What must I say?
> "I pray, sir" — Plague upon't! I cannot bring My tongue
> to such a pace. "Look, sir, my wounds! I got them in my
> country's service, when Some certain of your brethren
> roared and ran From the noise of our own drums."

Coriolanus would have enjoyed the 1992 and 2004 presidential campaigns. He would have found some aspects of them quite familiar. He would have well understood George H.W. Bush's ambivalence about comparing his valiant wartime military service with Bill Clinton's avoidance of the draft as he "roared and ran/From the noise of our own drums." Indeed, Bush's desultory campaign made him seem Coriolanus-like, especially when the voters "did hoot him out o' the city." Coriolanus would also have been amused by the irony of George W. Bush's swift-boating of John Kerry in 2004.

Coriolanus has something deep in common with George McGovern, who was one of the greatest war heroes ever to run for President. McGovern was awarded the Distinguished Flying Cross four times for his piloting thirty-five dangerous bombing runs over Nazi Germany during World War II. Yet in his speech accepting the 1972 Democratic Party nomination, McGovern, in a gesture Coriolanuss would have understood, deleted references to his war record. Like Coriolanus, McGovern did not want to boast of his war heroics. What makes this all the more ironic is that many Americans in the 1972 presidential campaign came to view McGovern—who opposed the Vietnam War—as a pacifist and even a coward.

Like some others who have tried to make the same switch in careers — Douglas MacArthur comes to mind — Coriolanus has more success as a soldier than as a politician. The Rome he returns to is riven with acrimonious class warfare. The plebeians are out of work, hungry, and in a rebellious mood. They are cynical and distrustful of a well-born war hero, who they fear will further exploit them. For his part, Coriolanus finds it difficult to curry favor with the plebeians just to get their votes. He hates the role of politician because he feels he is (oh my goodness!) not saying what he believes and, in grovelling for votes, is not acting naturally.

Egged on by two demagogues opposed to Coriolanus, the plebeians turn on the victor of Corioli. The demagogic tribunes of the people bait Coriolanus, who loses his temper and challenges them. Angered, he calls for their office as tribunes of the people to be abolished, for which he is charged with treason. The plebeians, egged on by their leaders, press for his punishment by death, but settle for his exile.

Coriolanus, bitter at his cruel treatment by his ungrateful countrymen, heads for the enemy Volscian camp and, to get even with his tormentors, offers to help his old adversaries destroy Rome. But at the last moment, after a tearful visit by his family, Coriolanus relents, refuses to wage war on Rome, and is killed by the Volscians, who realize that their plans of conquest are ruined.

Out of these events, Shakespeare crafted a play that has long been fairly unpopular. *Coriolanus* used to be one of the least frequently performed of the great Shakespeare plays, with few enthusiasts and admirers. Coriolanus is not a popular hero; he repels many who read or view the play. The most widely given reason for the play's unpopularity is the protagonist's anti-democratic attitude, his contempt for the common people. Playgoers do not like being sneered at.

And yet the last eighty years have seen renewed interest in *Coriolanus*. Starting in the 1930s, the play has become more popular, being performed more often and studied more carefully — as it should be. It is almost as if the political development of the twentieth century, with its heavy emphasis on the strengths and weaknesses of democracy, has breathed new theatrical life into *Coriolanus*. To an American reading the play during a presidential election, Coriolanus seems uncannily on point.

AN ANTI-DEMOCRATIC PLAY?

Much in *Coriolanus* justifies an anti-democratic reading. Coriolanus does not love the people. He and his patrician cohorts criticize the ordinary people, calling them rabble, mob, and even "rats." Although Coriolanus is portrayed as brave, great, and noble, the people are seen as stupid, ignorant, and fickle. Shakespeare does not even give the common people names; they are a faceless mob, a caricature, misled by demagogues. And after Coriolanus is exiled, Rome has no great man to defend it.

Some of this anti-democratic sentiment also shows through in *Julius Caesar*. In that much more famous and peremllially popular play, Marc Antony's funeral oration for the murdered Caesar depicts the perils of democracy and mob rule. Antony uses his speech to whip up the crowd to a frenzy. He tells them how Caesar in his will left money for each Roman citizen and his large private garden for the public. They should want revenge for his murder, Antony urges. Antony in that scene embodies that unscrupulous politician — the demagogue — who flatters, bribes, and misleads the people. That memorable scene is not an endorsement of government by the people.

If Alexander Hamilton ever read *Coriolanus*, he undoubtedly found it either congenial to his way of thinking or upsetting because of its unmasking of his own true elitest views. For *Coriolanus* gives a dramatic basis for Hamilton's notorious remark during Constitutional Convention of 1787 that, "Your people, sir — your people is a great beast." Eerily, the common people in *Coriolanus* are actually called "beasts." Hamilton's fellow Federalists often referred to the "swinish multitude" and used the terms "mob" and "people" interchangeably.

But to read *Coriolanus* as an anti-democratic play is to make a common mistake. It is just as easy to read an anti-aristocratic pro-democratic moral into *Coriolanus*. The play can be interpreted to mean that a leader insolent with power, who hates the common people, is dangerous to a republic. Coriolanus can be seen as an ambitious general who dislikes the people and, showing the same fickleness he criticizes in the people, goes over to the enemy when he is unable to achieve dictatorial power. Coriolanus thus becomes a traitor. On this reading, the play describes the evils of dictators and fascists, of men on horseback.

There is, however, a more complex yet more plausible explanation for the unpopularity of *Coriolanus*. If we look at *Coriolanus* unburdened by past criticism and received wisdom, we find another cause of its almost universal dislike. We find that such unpopularity may truly arise from the fundamental ambiguity of the play. For the play points in two opposite directions at the same time. A plain and fair view of *Coriolanus* supports both anti- and pro-democratic readings, aristocratic and republican, so that the resultant ambiguity leaves the audience, no matter what its bias, tense and dissatisfied. It is a problem play in which Shakespeare explores both points of view, exposing new facets of each, and leaves his unsettled audience finally in a state of ambivalence.

The tension and dissatisfaction induced in playgoers by *Coriolanus* accurately reflects the tension and dissatisfaction in the Rome depicted by Shakespeare. This Rome, early in the republic, is badly divided by class conflict, poor against rich, ruling classes versus oppressed classes. The very first scene of the play lifts up the curtain on such internal conflict as a group "of mutinous Citizens, with staves, clubs, and other weapons" gather to set the stage.

Shouts one of the armed, hungry, and angry plebeians to the rest: "You are all resolved to die rather than to famish?" The others answer: "Resolved, resolved." The apparent leader then announces: "First, you know Caius Marcius is chief enemy to the people." "We know't," is the joint answer. And the leader: "Let us kill him, and we'll have corn at our own price."

Thus the play starts off on a jarring note of class struggle, with plebeians venting their anger in a time of famine on the patrician who has denied them grain at cheap prices, and treated them with prideful contempt. This note is sustained throughout the first scene, until it becomes a general theme.

With a "we" versus "they" mind-set, the plebeians formulate their theory of class division:

> [T]he leanness that afflicts us, the object of our Misery, is as an inventory to particularize their abundance; our sufferance is a gain to them.

* * *

> They . . . suffer us to famish, and their storehouses crammed with grain; make edicts for usury, to support usurers; repeal daily any wholesome act established against the rich, and provide more piercing statutes daily to chain up and restrain the poor. If the wards eat us not up, they will.

Listen to the modern resonance of the plebeians' complaint. Do we not hear its echoes today? Are not politicians and lawmakers still accused of passing laws that favor the rich and hurt the poor? Is it not a constant theme in recent and current American politics? How many times do Democrats accuse Republicans of unwillingness to tax the wealthy? How often in recent years have we heard Republicans accuse Democrats of engaging in class warfare?

The basic ambiguity of *Coriolanus* can be traced to the troubles and discomforts of an important transition in political and constitutional thought: the transition to democracy. In the old days there were masters and slaves: masters decided what was to be done and liked their slaves, since slaves made them happy. The masters were of course quite happy with their lot. But all this changes with the inroads of democratic theory: slaves who had acquiesced before now ceased to do so; masters who had formerly no doubts of their rights now were hesitant and uncertain. Friction arose and caused unhappiness on both sides.

This troubling transition is in progress in *Coriolanus*, as we learn in the first scene. Already operating is the quasi-democratic custom of having a candidate for consul seek approval from the plebeians. On top of this custom, the Roman Senate, in response to the "complaining" of the plebeians, granted them a "petition" to have five tribunes "of their own choice." Now the plebeians for the first time would have tribunes of the people, democratically elected by the people themselves. Coriolanus calls this petition

> A strange one,
> To break the heart of generosity
> And make bold power look pale.

Caught in this political transition, Coriolanus is at a loss about how to cope with the new concept of democracy. He thinks the tribunes of the people will do no more than "defend their vulgar wisdoms"; he rages against the folly of ignorant plebeians having a role in government. "The rabble should have first unroofed the city," he adds,

> Ere so prevailed with me; it will in time
> Win upon power, and throw forth greater themes
> For insurrection's arguing.

Meninius, his patrician friend, portentously answers: "This is strange."

And so it is "strange" to those going through the transition. Coriolanus's distress and confusion about the plebeians' new democratic rights and where they will lead are the true introduction to the play's meaning. *Coriolanus* is a play that shows that while it is ongoing, the movement to democracy makes the world uncomfortable. Too often we forget how revolutionary an idea democracy is. This is something we should keep in mind when we talk about exporting democracy.

Transition to democracy can, in the short run, often create instability and chaos, as current world events in the Middle East and elsewhere show. For instance, in 2011, twenty years after the collapse of the Soviet Union, some Russians thought the change to democracy had not turned out exactly the way they had expected. Before the changes, they had only heard of or read about democracy, and thought it was a magical, beautiful word. But, according to the New York Times (Aug. 19, 2011), "In the decade the followed, chaotic social and economic changes as well as lurching attempts at reform gave democracy a bad name." Many people wished for stability and welcomed it under Vladimir Putin even at the cost of some democratic freedoms.

Insofar as *Coriolanus* is a play about the transition from aristocracy to democracy, it should have a peculiar appeal to Americans, for America symbolizes that transition, with all its difficulties. Alexis de Tocqueville's central proposition, almost an epiphany, was that by an irreversible design of Providence the American "democratic man" was bound to replace the dynastic "aristocracies" of Europe and in turn be embraced by the world. *Coriolanus* puts up a mirror to American politics. It is, as Garry Wills has written, "a work that speaks directly, and ominously, to the politics of our times."

The whole key that unlocks the play's underlying theme is in Coriolanus's lament about the uncertain struggle between democracy and aristocracy.

> my soul aches
> To know, when two authorities are up,
> Neither supreme, how soon confusion
> May enter 'twixt the gap of both and take
> The one by the other.

It is not only Coriolanus's soul that aches, but all humanity's.

It is an ache that we Americans still sometimes feel today. It shows up in the important though occasionally lost distinction between a republic and a democracy. "The believers in a democracy," writes David Brooks, "have unlimited faith in the character and judgment of the people and believe that political institutions should be responsive to their desires. The believers in a republic have large but limited faith in the character and judgment of the people and erect institutions and barriers to improve that character and guide that judgment." The tension between these two political beliefs has marked the history of America, and continues to do so.

American government has always blended the two political philosophies to form a democratic republic. The Founders were predominantly republicans. Our original Constitution, a product of fundamental compromise, had various checks and balances to offset popular majorities. The Senate, with two persons chosen by state legislatures representing each state regardless of population, is one familiar example. The Electoral College, which can sometime result in a president with fewer popular votes then a rival candidate, is another. There are many others.

But the balance between these concepts is not static. Sometimes one, sometimes the other has been in the ascendant. In recent years, republican values have somewhat yielded to democratic ones. The Constitution was amended to allow for direct election of U.S. Senators.

We are impatient and puzzled when, as in 2000, the presidential candidate with more popular votes loses to another candidate with fewer votes. Like the continents moving because of plate tectonics, the national mood shifts too, and the result today is that Americans often feel frustrated whenever their popular will is thwarted, regarding it as undemocratic and illegitimate.

Coriolanus shines a bright and illuminating beam on popular government. Shakespeare's comments about democracy are so honest, realistic, and perceptive that many people have thought that he favored the upper classes and lacked sympathy for the democratic ideal. But Shakespeare had compassion for ordinary people, though he hated the mob and the very idea of revolution. He was no populist. The play is a masterly exposition of a society starting to become democratic, with its problems as well as its attractions. The main theme of *Coriolanus* is, in various ways, the arrival of democracy and its prospects.

The arrival of democracy in the Rome of Coriolanus was anything but smooth, "It is a purposed thing," snaps Coriolanus,

> and grows by plot,
> To curb the will of the nobility;
> Suffer't and live with such as cannot rule
> Nor ever will be ruled.

Of the patrician legislators who gave in to the plebeian demands, Coriolanus sneeringly asks:

> Why,
> you grave but reckless senators, have you thus
> Given Hydra here to choose an officer . . .?

"In soothing them," adds Coriolanus fatefully, "we nourish 'gainst our Senate/The cockle of rebellion, insolence, sedition."

Coriolanus even casts doubt on the circumstances giving rise to the democratic reforms. He points out that the office of people's tribune was created only under threat of rebellion, "When what's not meet, but what must be, was law." From these rocky beginnings things get worse, to the point of civil war. "There hath been in Rome strange insurrections: the people against the senators, patricians, and nobles." As a result of Coriolanus's exile, reports one messenger, "The nobles . . . are in a ripe aptness to take all power from the people and to pluck from them their tribunes for ever."

That very suggestion — abolishing the office of people's tribune — pushed Coriolanus from his perch. For his anti-democratic attitude, he is found guilty of "manifest treason," and banished.

As for democracy's prospects, Shakespeare is remarkably clear eyed and prescient, but such candor and understanding do not make him an opponent of democracy, lest constructive criticism of anything we cherish be mistaken for disloyalty, opposition, or treason. But he does see many hidden dangers, dangers that threaten democracy itself, dangers we in the twenty-first century are all too familiar with. Shakespeare describes in *Coriolanus* some of the risks and hidden dangers of democratic forms being used to negate democracy.

Coriolanus's downfall results from power politics. The proximate cause of Coriolanus's descent was neither his pride nor his anti-democratic attitude, but the opposition to him by the people's tribunes. They plot to destroy Coriolanus because they see him as a rival and fear his power as consul. "Then our office may/During his power go sleep."

They rouse the people with demagoguery, telling them that Coriolanus is their "fixed enemy" and that he "will from them take/ Their liberties." Like many modern politicians, the two tribunes use popular prejudices and false claims and hollow promises to maintain their power. As Coriolanus chides the tribunes, "Have you not set them on?"

To achieve their end, the tribunes use modern pressure group tactics. Brutus and Sicinius, those false flatterers of the people, arrange to give the appearance of popular support by having their followers shout on cue when Coriolanus is challenged in the Forum. All of us have seen too many political conventions and gatherings orchestrated this way, we remember too many rallies and planned demonstrations, we have received too many requests to send identical telegrams to our political representatives.

Coriolanus demonstrates how hard it has been for a democracy to attract the best candidates for public office. Coriolanus is superbly qualified, a worthy and noble man, but one who cannot cope with political realities. No matter what his advisers tell him, or how well he knows he must control himself, Coriolanus finds it hard to give the plebeians a gesture of compromise. He shrinks from crowds and public platforms. He has been pushed into a political career for which he is temperamentally unfit.

This is not a phenomenon confined to the early Roman republic. There are those who think Eugene McCarthy, the Wisconsin senator who challenged President Johnson in the 1968 New Hampshire presidential primary but then later withdrew from the race, suffered from a Coriolanus-like inability to bend with the realities of politics. Some might argue that for much of the 1992 campaign George H.W. Bush balked, refusing with a stubborness born of a pride and overconfidence to do what a candidate must: retail himself and his policies through the tawdry practice of politics. Occasionally — under the stress of jeering hecklers — Bush broke his patrician-politician persona and angrily lashed out in a way reminiscent of Coriolanus. Much the same could be said of Al Gore — a stiff, uncomfortable, even awkward presidential candidate — in the 2000 campaign.

One reason able candidates are discouraged from running for elective office is a reluctance to demean themselves by acting out a charade during a campaign. In *Coriolanus* Shakespeare gives a scathing portrayal of the politician as disingenuous "actor." Seeking votes requires Coriolanus to play an uncomfortable role, to be something he is not. His fellow patricians tell proud Coriolanus that to be consul he must show his war wounds to the people and ask for their votes.

This he says he cannot do: "It is a part/That I shall blush in acting." No less than three times does playwright/actor Shakespeare use the metaphor of acting a theatrical role to describe what Coriolanus must do as a politician. But Coriolanus despised toadying to the masses.

Where Coriolanus's male political advisers are indirect, his mother is forthright in counselling him to be devious. She tells him to speak "such words that are but roted in/Your tongue, though but bastards and syllables/Of no allowance to your bosom's truth." "Tell the voters whatever they want to hear," is the essence of his mother's advice. Move over, Karl Rove and Roger Ailes.

If Shakespeare's portrayal of dissembling by political candidates rings true, then we have to reconsider how we choose between those running for office. Perhaps we have to discount or, better yet, disregard just about everything said by any candidate during an election campaign. Whatever a candidate says about election issues is suspect, because it may be designed for the sole purpose of getting votes from a particular group, only to be forgotten the morning after election day, like "Read my lips, no new taxes."

A truer test must be the candidate's total character, personality, positions, and performance up to the point of becoming a candidate. This is not limited to the famous character issue that figured so prominently in the 1992 campaign, but a much broader assessment of performance as opposed to promises. That is how a bettor plays the horses; he or she looks at the scratch sheet, not at what the owner or the jockey says that morning. *Coriolanus* warns us to pay less attention than we do to what a politician says in the heat of a campaign, and instead to look at his or her political scratchsheet, actual deeds not mere words.

To be sure, Shakespeare's *Coriolanus* does expose basic problems in a democracy, never more so than when a Roman citizen moans, "We willingly consented to his banishment, yet it was against our will." Exactly what does this statement mean? Here Shakespeare exposes unsolved issues of popular government: not merely superficial questions of the people's fickleness, but conundrums going to the heart of political philosophy, like Rousseau's problematical "general will." Alexander Bickel, a leading constitutional law scholar who died too young in 1973 at the age of forty-nine, dealt with some of these issues in his last book, *The Morality of Consent*. He argued that "consent and stability are not produced by" popular elections, that "the people are something else than a majority registered on election day." Although Bickel was using the writings of Edmund Burke as a touchstone for studying current issues in American constitutional theory, his comments nonetheless help explain what the disenchanted Roman citizen in *Coriolanus* meant.

For Shakespeare to limn some of democracy's dangers does not necessarily make him an opponent of popular government. Nor does it make him unduly pessimistic about the prospects for democracy. On the contrary, awareness of flaws helps us guard against evil men seeking to take advantage of them. The rise of fascism and communism in the last century is in no small part due to sinister use of democracy's weaknesses to destroy democracy.

Coriolanus, as drawn by Shakespeare, is no ideal democratic leader. He is described as "insolent, o'ercome with pride, ambitious past all thinking,/Self-loving."

The text of the play suggests the possibility that Coriolanus wanted to become a dictator, "affecting one sole throne without assistance." Although at least Menenius says, "I think not so," (4.6.41-42), another

Roman says, "Rome/Sits safe and still without" Coriolanus. A leader who dislikes his people is no real democratic leader.

Shakespeare's answers are often ambiguous, particularly to the question whether he was for or against democracy. He dramatizes issues rather than answers. And yet the true Shakespeare, common man of the people who rose by talent and ability to prominence, may speak through one of the tribunes who says, in words still reverberating throughout the world, "the people must have their voices."

CORIOLANUS VERSUS THE LAW

Though perhaps not obvious on a first reading, the more we study *Coriolanus* the more we understand where it fits in the world of legal literature. *Coriolanus* is a precursor of modern works of fiction dealing with fundamental cultural themes. The nexus between *Coriolanus* and modern literature emerges from the analysis offered by Richard Weisberg in his 1984 book *The Failure of the Word*. Weisberg, a professor at Cardozo Law School in Manhattan, does not discuss *Coriolanus*; he focuses on the relationship between modern cultural malaise and the lawyer-like protagonists in nineteenth and twentieth-century literature by authors such as Dostoyevsky, Flaubert, Camus, and Melville. But to set forth Weisberg's theory is to show why it embraces *Coriolanus* too.

According to Weisberg, the use of lawyer-like protagonists in modern literature is the key to understanding basic aspects of modern culture. In such characters are combined the twin themes of *ressentiment* and legalism. These themes, in turn, combine to produce the "legalistic *ressentiment*" that Weisberg regards as so central to modern fiction.

At the heart of Weisberg's literary analysis lies the concept of *ressentiment*. That concept, which Weisberg attributes to Neitzsche, means perpetual rancor, and it involves disguised rage taking the form of public "revenge" against imagined "insults." Ressentient individuals have a lingering sense of injury without a firm sense of values. They generally feel a discrepancy between what they consider their own worth to be and the actual worth and position accorded them by others.

Ressentiment is, for Weisberg, "modern Western culture's own deepest malaise. To understand *ressentiment* and ressentient injustice is to understand law and language today," says Weisberg. *Ressentiment* is a "negative force in society and history," and plays a major role in the novels that he interprets. In each literary work examined by Weisberg,

85

ressentiment mars the protagonist. And in each such work of fiction, the protagonist is a lawyer or lawyer-like character.

These fictional lawyer-types, flawed by *ressentiment*, are the bridge to Weisberg's other major theme: legalism. These literary legal figures have several other distinctive traits. Weisberg describes the lawyer-like protagonists as well-educated, hard working, insightful individuals, blessed with subtle and careful minds, endowed with superior powers of perception, and distinctively articulate at their best. Weisberg sees these fictional lawyer-types, at their worst, as avoiding and distorting reality and life, as maladjusted, repressed, and violent individuals who adhere to resentful values. They are inactive, promoters of injustice, indirect with hidden motives, equivocating, and dissembling (and above all too wordy). This verbosity is a primary trait.

Juxtaposed against the predominantly negative traits of lawyer figures are the primarily attractive qualities of the "just individual." Such an individual, while nonverbal and less articulate, is more popular, basically well adjusted, and fulfilled. He has a keen intelligence and couples action with reason. Unlike his verbose legal counterpart, the just individual responds quickly and effectively to evil, though nonverbally. He is associated with happiness, power, beauty, goodness, and other positive forms of life. He spontaneously partakes of life.

Tension between these two sets of character traits generates the energy for Weisberg's thesis. According to that thesis, the bitter and resentful verbosity, the sheer wordiness, of fictional lawyers has produced what Weisberg sees as the prevailing failure of modern Western culture. Speech is an inadequate replacement for legitimate action. Yet we have been plagued by the "futile wordiness of legalistic protagonists." Hence the genesis of Weisberg's title, *The Failure of the Word*, and his subtitle, *The Protagonist as Lawyer in Modern Fiction*.

Weisberg's analysis helps us to understand *Coriolanus* in a non-traditional way. In Shakespeare's play, Coriolanus's conflict with the tribunes of the people can be seen as a clash between the non-verbal man of action and the bitter and resentful verbosity of the legalistic tribunes of the people. Unlike, say, Hamlet, Coriolanus is a man of deeds, not words. As Coriolanus describes himself, "Yet oft/When blows have made me stay, I fled from words." Coriolanus lived the motto — "Deeds Not Words" — of the U.S. Army's 92nd Infantry Division, the now famous segregated, courageous "Buffalo Soldiers" of World War II.

But Coriolanus's lack of verbal facility lands him in trouble. Like Billy

Budd in Melville's story, Coriolanus also does not speak when he should speak, as when he refuses to talk to potential voters. And then when he does speak, he says the wrong thing, as when he rages against the folly of letting ignorant plebeians have a voice in the government. Words taunt him. He is confused and enraged by words like "shall," "traitor," and "boy." When he verbally abuses the commoners, one of their tribunes shouts at Coriolanus, "No more words. We beseech you."

By contrast, Coriolanus's political enemies — the verbally skilled tribunes of the people — wrap themselves in the law. Unlike Coriolanus, who is an unpracticed orator, the tribunes of the people excel in public speaking, in manipulating crowds, in bending the Roman people to their will. But, as we lawyers know only too well, just because someone can argue better does not mean he or she is right. The tribunes resent Coriolanus and conspire to ruin him. When Coriolanus falls into the trap set for him and dares to suggest that the tribunes lose their job, he is challenging "the people's magistrates." What is Coriolanus's great crime? "[H]e hath resisted law." Coriolanus has set himself up against the law.

DUE PROCESS

In clashing with the law, Coriolanus tests the law's most basic boast: fairness. The play stresses the bedrock importance of due process of law as a bulwark against mob passion. After Coriolanus suggests that the office of tribune be eliminated, the tribunes manipulate the crowds, who shout, "Down with him, down with him!" The tribunes would deny Coriolanus any procedural rights:

> he hath resisted law,
> And therefore law shall scorn him further trial
> Than the severity of the public power,
> Which he so sets at naught.

Above the cacophony of the crowd, a voice of reason tries to make itself heard. "Proceed by process," exclaims patrician Menenius, in an effort to bring the mob to its senses. "Give me leave, I'll go to him and undertake to bring him/Where he shall answer by a lawful form."

This incident in *Coriolanus* calls to mind other pleas for process by another patrician — Boston Brahmin Oliver Wendell Holmes, Jr., who sat on the United States Supreme Court from 1902 to 1932. One such plea came in a 1915 dissent in a Supreme Court case involving the notorious trial of Leo Frank, convicted of murdering a girl who worked in a Georgia pencil factory that he managed. The "trial" took place amid intense anti-Semitism and Southern hatred of "foreigners" from New York (Frank was a New York Jew).

When the Supreme Court denied Leo Frank's habeas corpus petition, Holmes dissented and, sounding like Menenius, stated: "Whatever disagreement there may be as to the scope of the phrase 'due process of law,' there can be no doubt that it embraces the fundamental conception of a fair trial, with opportunity to be heard." Mob law is not due process of law, especially where, as Holmes wrote for the Court in a later case, "the whole proceeding is a mask [where] counsel, jury, and judge were swept to the fatal end by an irresistible wave of public passion."

So important is this theme in *Coriolanus* that it repeats itself in the play's last scene, after the Volscians discover that Coriolanus has made an unauthorized peace with Rome. The Volscian people, like the Roman people before them, are stirred up against Coriolanus to destroy him. "Let him die for't." "Tear him to pieces." Once again Coriolanus is accused of treason, just as he was in Rome. And once again, there is the restraining plea: "His last offenses to us/Shall have judicious hearing."

THE PARABLE OF THE BELLY

The political core of *Coriolanus* is the scene containing the famous Parable of the Belly. One of the most memorable scenes in all Shakespeare, it forms the basis of many critics' views that the Bard opposed democracy. Menenius Agrippa, a patrician friend of Coriolanus with a reputation as a well-meaning liberal, tells the fable to mollify the hungry and rebellious plebeians.

Another look at Menenius's tale, however, may reveal a very different but no less important meaning. From this alternative viewpoint, the Parable of the Belly unmasks Menenius as a deceitful and hypocritical apologist for Rome's aristocratic class structure. We may discover that Menenius's understanding of the parable as a way to lull the lower classes into quiet acceptance of the status quo was completely ill conceived. If the parable is correctly understood, it does contain a genuine and useful theory of democracy.

Menenius tells the parable in the first scene of the first act. Starved, angry, and armed plebeians gather to speak of revolution against the upper classes. As they plot, Menenius comes upon them. When the plebeians first see Menenius, they immediately contrast him to Coriolanus. Only a few moments before, they called Coriolanus the "chief enemy to the people," while they refer to Menenius as "one that hath always loved the people."

This "lover of the people" sees trouble brewing, and tries to turn the plebeians away from their violent plans. "Why, masters, my good friends, mine honest neighbors,/Will you undo yourselves?" asks Menenius. The leader of the plebeians shouts back, "We cannot, sir, we are undone already." To this pithy retort, Menenius responds in a curious way for "one that hath always loved the people."

He begins by saying, "I tell you, friends, most charitable care/Have the patricians of you." If there is economic hardship, "the gods, not the patricians, make it," and Menenius tells the plebeians to pray. In any event, rebellion will be futile; "you may as well/Strike at the heaven with your staves as lift them/Against the Roman state," which will crush you. "You slander/The helms o' the state [*i.e.*, we patricians], who care for you like fathers."

The plebeians are not buying what Menenius is selling. "Care for us!" cries out the plebeian leader sardonically. This outspoken common citizen then proceeds to show with eloquence how the plight of the plebeians results not from the gods but from the patricians. Instantly we think of another Shakespeare play about Rome — *Julius Caesar* — in which a character points out how "The fault, dear Brutus, is not in our stars,/But in ourselves."

Now Menenius says: "I shall tell you/A pretty tale." A famished plebeian sings out, "You must not think to fob off our disgrace with a tale." But Menenius nonetheless goes ahead with his story of the revolt of the other parts of the body against the belly because, while they were busy working for the general good, the belly was lazy in the middle of the body, hoarding the food.

"There was a time," recounts Menenius, "when all the body's members/Rebell'd against the belly." They accused the belly of being "idle and inactive," of doing nothing but having the pleasure of getting the food first, "never bearing/Like labor with the rest." In contrast to the belly, the other parts of the body

> Did see and hear, devise, instruct, walk, feel
> And, mutually participate, did minister

Unto the appetite and affection common
of the whole body.

"With a kind of smile," the belly

tauntingly replied
To the discontented members, the mutinous parts
That envied his receipt; even so most fitly
As you malign our senators for that
They are not such as you.

This tell-tale taunt in the form of a smile is a vital and explicit clue not only to the belly's true point of view, but also to the underlying intentions of Menenius.

Perhaps realizing his slip, Menenius immediately alters the belly's aspects from taunting and smiling to grave and deliberate, to make it less obviously sarcastic and derisive. According to Menenius, "Your most grave belly was deliberate, / Not rash like his accusers, and thus answered":

"True is it, my incorporate friends," quoth he,
"That I receive the general food at first
Which you do live upon; and fit it is,
Because I am the storehouse and the shop
Of the whole body. But, if you do remember,
I send it through the rivers of your blood,
Even to the court, the heart, to the seat o' the brain;
And, through the cranks and offices of man,
The strongest nerves and small inferior veins
From me receive that natural competency
Whereby they live. And though that all at once,
You, my good friends, . . . cannot
See what I do deliver out to each,
Yet I can make my audit up, that all
from me do back receive the flour of all,
And leave me but the bran."

A citizen asks Menenius to explain the meaning of the parable. "The senators of Rome are this good belly," answers Menenius,

And you the mutinous members; for, examine
Their counsels and their cares, digest things rightly
Touching the weal o' the common, and you shall find
No public benefit which you receive
But it proceeds or comes from them to you,
And no way from yourselves.

The explanation given by Menenius — Shakespeare does not say if Menenius smiled tauntingly as he explained — is transparently self-serving. To Menenius, the Roman patricians, like the belly, are altruistic. They have a hard job providing benefits to all, but they valiantly do the best they can. The fountainhead of Roman welfare, they ask for nothing in return. The rest of the body politic get the "flour," the patricians get the "bran." How could the ungrateful plebeians even think of rebelling against the selfless patricians, who are moved solely by devotion to the interests of others?

When scrutinized, however, Menenius's interpretation of the parable is anything but democratic. In essence, it is, in the now familiar language of supply-side economics, a trickle-down theory. We immediately recognize it as the deceptive and fallacious logic used since the beginning of time by the powerful and the privileged in all ages to justify their status, however originally gotten. As Harold Goddard put it so well thirty years before Ronald Reagan's first term as president: "If only we are prosperous, some of our prosperity is bound to trickle down to you. Let the stomach flourish and the smallest capillaries will be nourished."

With this "organic tale," the patricians, under color of the common good, used the plebeians for the patricians' own greedy purposes. In his controversial but popular book *The Closing of the American Mind*, Allan Bloom refers to the tale as "one of the myths of rulership that protected corrupt and selfish regimes." It is remarkable that the Parable of the Belly has not been openly discussed in recent American elections.

Hazlitt's comment in the early 1800s caught Menenius's meaning exactly. The parable, wrote Hazlitt, means that those who have little shall have less, and that those who have much shall take all the others have left. The people are poor; therefore they ought to be starved. They are slaves; therefore they ought to be beaten. They work hard; therefore they ought to be treated like beasts of burden. They are ignorant; therefore they ought not to be allowed to feel that they want food, or clothing, or rest, that they are enslaved, oppressed, and miserable.

Seen for what it is, the Parable of the Belly exposes Menenius as a fake democrat, a political hypocrite. As the parable shows, Menenius is an unreconstructed conservative aristocrat. His true anti-democratic leanings break through again when a plebeian interrupts him during his telling of the tale. "What then?" blurts out Menenius, "Fore me, this fellow speaks!" Menenius will not have any commoner before him.

And if there were any doubt, Menenius betrays himself as soon as he finishes his story. He tells the plebeians: "Rome and her rats are at the point of battle." Who are these rats? The plebeians.

He who had supposedly always loved the people reveals himself, in fact, to be the opposite. He jeers at them and mocks them. "There have been many great men," observes a keen plebeian at another point, "that have flattered the people who ne'er loved them." More than the forthright Coriolanus, Menenius is really the "chief enemy to the people."

But there is another, more positive interpretation of the Parable of the Belly. The comparison of the body to the body politic is one of the oldest in human thought. Rightfully understood, the fable contains profound political and social wisdom. This wisdom flows from the idea of mutual participation referred to in the Parable:

> the other instruments
> Did see and learn, devise, instruct, walk, feel
> And, *mutually participate*, did minister
> Unto the appetite and affection common
> Of the whole body.

The concept of mutual participation is a fine expression of the democratic ideal. It is embodied in the social contract theories of Hobbes and Locke, published less than a century after Shakespeare wrote. Under these theories, the ruled are not subjected by nature to the rulers; the rulers do not naturally care only for the good of the ruled. All choose, by mutual participation, to form a society and a government.

This choice was behind the founding of America. In *Federalist No. 22*, Alexander Hamilton wrote, "The fabric of American empire ought to rest on the solid basis of THE CONSENT OF THE PEOPLE. The stream of national power ought to flow immediately from that pure, original fountain of all legitimate authority." In *No. 49*, Madison said, "[T]he people are the only legitimate fountain of power." And in *No.*

40, he commented that the convention's proposal was to be submitted "*to the people themselves*" because they are "this supreme authority."

Today, the old concept of mutual participation is at the center of an important debate in political philosophy. Contemporary liberal philosophers, such as John Rawls, Ronald Dworkin and Robert Nozick, focus on individual rights with a moderate vision of community. Their intellectual adversaries, such as Michael Sandel, Michael Walzer and Alisdair MacIntyre, are called communitarians because they stress obligations to the community, to shared virtues and common purposes. Each side charges the other with insufficiently protecting certain values, but both are really working out a modern democratic view of mutual participation. Out of this current debate may evolve a new wrinkle in the Parable of the Belly.

Analyzed from this perspective, the Parable of the Belly proves the opposite of what it is usually cited for. It is usually relied on to show Shakespeare's prejudice in favor of the upper classes and his lack of sympathy for the common people and the democratic ideal. But, properly understood in context, the fable demonstrates precisely the contrary.

GOVERNMENT OF THE PEOPLE

We cannot get *Coriolanus* out of our minds. It grabs our attention and refuses to let go. It disturbs, it troubles, it makes us uncomfortable by the way it portrays a society's transition to democracy. Shakespeare forces us to reexamine some of our most cherished political myths, including the doctrine that all power arises from the people.

Coriolanus leaves us unsure about what popular government really means. We see the unresolved political and economic tensions between the wealthy and powerful patricians, on one hand, and the poor, weak, but far more numerous plebeians on the other. To alleviate such tension, pre-existing custom requires popular approval for someone seeking the high office of consul. Most of the time, we get the impression such popular approval was a mere formality in the oligarchic Rome of Coriolanus, and that impression bothers us. It bothers us because we start to ask ourselves whether the formality of popular approval is not what it seems.

Surely the custom of popular approval for the office of consul failed to make ancient Rome a democracy. On the contrary, the plebeians felt it necessary to demand the right to their own representatives — five people's tribunes. Having wrung that concession from the ruling patricians in the Senate, the plebeians well understood that the patricians were still very much in control of things. We ask ourselves if there is not some deeper and timeless lesson here.

Menenius's disingenuous interpretation of the Parable of the Belly only increases our discomfort. There we recognize a ruling class effort to devise a false theory of popular sovereignty to shore up and legitimize an oligarchic regime. That the tale is told by a supposed friend of the people only makes matters worse. We ask ourselves how many such fictions have been palmed off on the people throughout history.

When the new tribunes of the people finally exercise their power, we look hopefully for signs of democratic progress, but are disappointed. We find the people's tribunes manipulating the people for the tribunes' own objectives, much as the patricians had done for the patricians' purposes. Instead of the patricians ruling the people, now we have the people's tribunes ruling the people — and doing so, what is more, in the very name of the people! In both situations we see the many being ruled by the few, and we ask ourselves if that is not always the case, even when popular sovereignty is supposed to be the source of all power.

We wonder if the troubling questions about popular government raised by *Coriolanus* apply to our own time and place. We wonder if the idea of popular self-government, a presupposition of the American political order, is, as in *Coriolanus*, a myth. After all, the "self" of self-government has always been a controversial issue in constitutional theory. We wonder about theories of political legitimacy, about the character and sources of political authority in America.

Debate over the foundations of American political order is largely a debate over the nature of constitutional law. Into the vessel of the Constitution we pour our national debate over the nature of legitimate political authority.

Over twenty years ago, Ronald Reagan gave us a typical statement of the ruling myth. In his farewell address to the nation in January 1989, Reagan paid traditional homage to our democratic form of self-government. "Ours was the first revolution in the history of mankind," he said, "that truly reversed the course of government, and with three little words: 'We the People.'"

The outgoing President continued: "'We the People' tell the Government what to do, it doesn't tell us. 'We the People' are the driver — the Government is the car. And we decide where it should go, and by what route, and how fast. Almost all the world's constitutions are documents in which governments tell the people what their privileges are. Our constitution is a document in which 'We the People' tell the Government what it is allowed to do. 'We the People' are free."

Then the President wound up this part of his speech with a statement of his credo. "This belief," he said, referring to government by the people, "has been the underlying basis for everything I tried to do these past eight years." But the "belief" in government by the people is more than Mr. Reagan's private faith. It has been the "underlying basis for everything" in American political mythology.

Political legitimacy in the modern nation-state depends upon popular sovereignty. One of the "self-evident truths" in the Declaration of Independence described governments as "deriving their just powers from the consent of the governed." The *Federalist Papers* echoed the same thought.

But *Coriolanus* makes us question the true meaning of these self-evident truths. A 1988 book, *Inventing the People* by eminent historian Edmund Morgan, asks more such probing questions. Morgan starts with David Hume's observation that most of us submit willingly to be governed by a few of us. Most of us obey the government under which we find ourselves. Most of us submit neither out of fear nor out of conscience, but rather through unreflective habit.

All government, writes Morgan, "rests on the consent, however obtained, of the governed." Tacit agreement of the subjects has always been necessary, even for authoritarian rulers. Since force is not enough, "over the long run," to induce consent, something else is needed to make the many submit to the few. Acquiescence is usually secured not by a show of force, but by propagating a theory or fiction that gives the ruler legitimacy. Political leaders thus must persuade the many to submit to government by the few. "The success of government thus requires the acceptance of fictions."

In short, Morgan says,

> government requires make-believe. Make believe that the king is divine, make believe that he can do no wrong or make believe that the voice of the people is the voice of god. Make believe that the people *have* a voice or make believe that the representatives of the people *are*

95

the people. Make believe that the governors are the servants of the people.

To acknowledge that we rely so heavily on make-believe is a little uncomfortable. So, as Morgan points out, we generally call the fictions by some more exalted names. "We may proclaim them as self-evident truths, and that designation is not inappropriate, for it implies our commitment to them and at the same time protects them from challenge." Self-evident propositions are not debatable, and to challenge them would rend the fabric of society. The divine right of kings readily strikes us as a fiction; popular sovereignty seems less fictional to us.

The few who govern take care to nourish those fictions providing the few with justification for their government of the many and reconciling the many to that government. Those fictions are necessary; we cannot live without them; nor should we scoff at them. But the fictions needed to make the many submit to the few are often at variance with observable fact. Practices that look like popular sovereignty in reality are subject to manipulation, particularly by "leaders" who know how to manipulate the political process.

Morgan's thesis is that the fictional qualities of popular sovereignty actually sustain rather than threaten the human values associated with it. He points out how the fictions may often mold the real world. To prevent the collapse of the fictions, we move the facts to fit the fiction (for example, voting rights laws, lowering voting age), we make our world conform more closely to what we want it to be. And the governing few may also find themselves limited by the fictions on which their authority depends.

The central problem of popular sovereignty is just this: setting limits to a government deriving its authority from a people for whom it claims the sole right to speak. It is the problem of the people exercising effective control over a government pretending to speak for them. It is the problem of reconciling the wishes, needs and rights of actual people with the overriding will of a fictional sovereign people.

Some of the characters in *Coriolanus* recognize these limitations. After the people's tribunes achieve their goal of banishing Coriolanus, one of them says:

> Now we have shown our power,
> Let us seem humbler after it is done

Than when it was a-doing.

Perhaps most insightful of all is the comment by Aufidias, leader of the hated Volscians, who sees into the heart of democratic government when he says: "We must proceed as we do find the people."

Coriolanus may well be, as Garry Wills says, Shakespeare's "most sophisticated political creation." It scrutinizes and examines the impact of democracy from several points of view. It reveals in a particular context the fiction of popular sovereignty serving to legitimize the rule not of the people, but of a small and privileged elite. Despite populist rhetoric in ancient Rome, the few continued to rule the many, just as they always had done.

Coriolanus compels us to think again about the meaning of government of the people. It makes us dig beneath the surface of political catchphrases and myths. From the perspective of political theory, *Coriolanus* is a delight. And, as Hazlitt wrote in his essay on *Coriolanus* in the early nineteenth century, "we may depend upon it that what men delight to read in books, they will put in practice in reality." It is good to remember Hazlitt's comment as we contemplate democracy and the rule of law in America.

CHAPTER 5

The Case of the Unmentioned Charter
(King John)

One of the many sources of American democracy and the rule of law is of course Magna Carta. The Great Charter has an honored place in the history of liberty, which makes its absence from Shakespeare's play about King John, the monarch who was forced to grant Magna Carta, intriguing.

What is omitted sometimes tells more than what is said. No less a sleuth than Sherlock Holmes once famously pointed this out when a dog failed to bark. In "Silver Blaze," Holmes and Dr. Watson investigate a farm where mysterious things have happened. A police inspector and Holmes have the following exchange:

"Is there any point to which you would wish to draw my attention?"

"To the curious incident of the dog in the night-time."

"The dog did nothing in the night-time."

"That was the curious incident," remarked Sherlock Holmes.

A similarly curious incident occurs in Shakespeare's *King John*, one of the Bard's minor and rarely performed plays. Minor and rarely performed though it may be, *King John* has an important link to legal history, but that link is not immediately obvious, until our attention is drawn to what the play mysteriously fails to say.

By far the most memorable event in King John's reign, as far as posterity is concerned, was the granting of Magna Carta in 1215. No other single document has had as long and as powerful an influence on the legal concepts of the English-speaking peoples. It is the document that first explicitly prevented government from depriving someone of his or her life, liberty, or property without due process of law. The famous language in Chapter 29 of Magna Carta is: "No freeman shall be taken or imprisoned, or disseised of his free tenement, liberties or free customs, or outlawed or exiled or in any wise destroyed . . . unless by lawful judgment of his peers, or by the law of the land." In historical significance, signing Magna Carta, a great landmark on the road to law and liberty, dwarfs anything else King John did.

For all its significance, however, Magna Carta goes completely unmentioned in Shakespeare's play about King John.

Such a mysterious and glaring omission has over the years drawn criticism down around Shakespeare's head. Even today, basic questions still nag at us. How could such a great playwright, in a play about an unpopular and oppressive king, fail to portray or even discuss the first basic charter of English freedom? Why would Shakespeare, who showed no reluctance to use controversial facts from the reigns of more recent monarchs in his histories, shy away from any reference at all to Magna Carta in *King John*? Why was it left out?

To try to solve this curious mystery, we need to act a little like a detective. We need to imagine how Sherlock Holmes would approach the "case of the unmentioned charter."

At the outset, the famous detective would probably dispose of existing theories. He would dismiss the theory that Shakespeare did not regard the Charter "as good theater," since it is hard to imagine a scene with more dramatic potential than a monarch reluctantly yielding power to avoid civil war. We can easily conceive the playwright describing the extraordinary scene at Runnymede with the English lords and high churchmen, joined by representatives of the City of London, gathered on the great meadow requiring John to confirm and guarantee their historic liberties. Knowing that Shakespeare depicts John as weak, indecisive, and cruel, Holmes would probably find unpersuasive the argument that including Magna Carta would have spoiled the supposed contrary dramatic effect of King John as a champion of England against foreign influences.

Equally flawed is the theory that Shakespeare's omission stems from his plagiarism of another play, which later scholarship has shown came after, and not before, Shakespeare's effort. Nor would Holmes seriously credit Shakespeare's omission of Magna Carta as "politically discreet" in view of his nasty portrait of King John and Shakespeare's many plays about revolts against English kings and murders of political leaders.

Having weighed and rejected these existing theories, Holmes might look for clues in the relevant chronology. We know that Magna Carta was granted in 1215. We also know that Shakespeare wrote *King John* in the 1590s. And we know too that we are looking at this mystery from the vantage point of twenty-first-century Americans. Hidden in these dates, what occurred between them, and the changes in attitudes over time may lie the answer to the fundamental riddle of *King John*.

About a century after 1215, a strange thing happened to Magna Carta. As Magna Carta settled into the foundations of English law and government, it lost its unique status and became mere "law." In many ways it was neglected and ignored, covered over and forgotten in the strife of the fifteenth and sixteenth centuries. In those turbulent centuries, Parliament and the courts found Magna Carta largely irrelevant. The Charter's rhetoric of liberty under law had been used so much that it became a cliché. Lawyers who made arguments based on Magna Carta were criticized for taking "frivolous exceptions."

This is not to say that Magna Carta entirely disappeared from view. Collections of statutes always began with Magna Carta. It was cited in court cases from time to time. But its role was greatly diminished. As Winston Churchill put it in the first volume of his *History of the English Speaking Peoples*, "Little more was heard of the Charter until the seventeenth century."

The centuries-long partial eclipse of Magna Carta explains more convincingly than anything else why Shakespeare omitted it in *King John*.

In the 1590s, as Shakespeare was writing the play, Magna Carta was still suffering from general neglect. Magna Carta never meant to Shakespeare what it means to us, or even what it meant to his own countrymen half a century later. It is not that Shakespeare "forgot" about Magna Carta, but that in his day Magna Carta was almost moribund. From Shakespeare's striking omission, we can deduce a lack of special interest on the part of Englishmen in Magna Carta at the end of the sixteenth century.

All that changed shortly after Shakespeare's death in 1616. As the abuses of the Stuarts grew, Magna Carta enjoyed a phenomenal revival at the critical moment in English history. Led by former Chief Justice Edward Coke and other lawyers who were not what we now call "originalists," Parliament in the 1620s invoked Magna Carta as "fundamental law" governing the constitutional relationship between the political nation and James I and Charles I. Those opposed to Stuart encroachment upon liberty rediscovered Magna Carta and made of it a rallying cry against oppression.

Magna Carta's great role during the seventeenth-century struggle between Parliament and the Stuarts was its high-water mark in English consciousness. It started an enduring myth about the Great Charter as a document protecting the basic liberties of all citizens. Ignoring the original intent and text of Magna Carta as designed to protect the barons and not ordinary subjects, to enhance feudalism not democracy, the new myth saw Magna Carta as a link with the supposed ancient laws and liberties of Anglo-Saxon times. Magna Carta came to symbolize constitutional monarchy and the idea of law standing even above the king and arbitrary rule by one man. These concepts were heady drafts, and form the core of what we have come to think of Magna Carta.

But Magna Carta's actual role in English law changed with English history. By the time of the Restoration of Charles II in 1660, Magna Carta had done its work as a mighty instrument of liberty. England turned away from constitutionalism based on fundamental law, and returned to constitutionalism dependent on the rule of law, the preservation of liberties by the working of law that was less than fundamental law. Magna Carta assumed its more modest role of mere "law," protecting the property of the subject and the liberty of his person. British constitutionalism, allowing for the protection of liberties by the rule of law, had discredited both a written instrument and fundamental law and come to rest upon restrained, customary, political activity in a democratically elected House of Commons.

In America, however, the experience with Magna Carta was very different. When the English first colonized America in the 1600s, they brought with them the expansive idea, the myth, of Magna Carta then prevalent in the political life of the mother country. This mind-set created an attitude toward constitutionalism in America, reinforced by colonial charters. In building their new political entities, the colonists in America tried to preserve the laws and liberties of Englishmen. Unlike England, America never retired Magna Carta.

On the contrary, as Magna Carta waned in importance and practical applicability in eighteenth-century England, it grew in strength in America. It became a bulwark against imperial abuses. It was frequently cited by leaders of the American Revolution. Magna Carta was an inspiration for the Declaration of Independence and the Constitution and our Bill of Rights. It is a vital part of our history and our legal traditions. The English in America were more attached to Magna Carta than the English in England.

These differences in attitude persist. Down even to today, Americans fervently revere Magna Carta more so than do most Englishmen. The only monument at Runnymede dedicated to Magna Carta was erected not by the English but by Americans — the American Bar Association, to be precise — in 1957. The simple legend on the monument states: "To commemorate Magna Carta, symbol of freedom under law."

With this history, the mystery of the unmentioned charter is solved. As twenty-first-century Americans, we understandably ask why Shakespeare omitted Magna Carta — that great symbol — from *King John*. But the answer comes through fairly clearly. What is a great symbol of freedom under law to us today did not achieve that special status in England until the mid-seventeenth century. To Shakespeare writing at the end of the sixteenth century, before the struggle between Parliament and the Stuarts, Magna Carta was not nearly so significant, if indeed it was regarded as anything special at all.

Therefore, we can infer that Shakespeare was unaware that he was excluding anything important in writing *King John* the way he did. We should not judge Shakespeare's sixteenth-century understanding by different twenty-first-century standards. We do better by using it as a mirror of the general understanding of his contemporaries.

Criticizing Shakespeare for omitting Magna Carta from *King John* — as many do — is like criticizing late nineteenth-century American constitutional lawyers for not making arguments based on the Due Process or Equal Protection Clauses of the Fourteenth Amendment or on the anti-discrimination provisions of the original Civil Rights Acts, which were sleeping giants until modern times.

Neither Shakespeare nor we can always predict what will be the next sleeping legal giant to awake.

CHAPTER 6

Shakespeare's Crooked Judges

Magna Carta also bears on that sin of sins — the crooked judge. "To none will we sell, deny, or delay right or justice," declares Magna Carta in no uncertain terms. It is a good rule that has come down through the ages and runs through Shakespeare's plays.

The more we read Shakespeare, the more we see him as timeless, which is one of the reasons we like him so much. The four centuries between us shrink to nothing. Times change, but far more so than human nature. Today's news is filled, from time to time, with scandal about a judge accused of selling justice. Shakespeare treats the theme of the crooked judge, and he does so more than once.

At the start of *Richard II*, for instance, the king sits in judgment of his cousin Bolingbroke and the Duke of Norfolk. Bolingbroke accuses Norfolk of murdering the Duke of Gloucester, who in fact had been murdered at King Richard's orders. Does Richard disqualify himself as judge either on the ground that he will favor his family relation or on the other ground of participation in the crime? No. He protests, a bit overmuch perhaps, how "impartial are our eyes and ears."

The stress on the theme of judicial bias shows up again later in the play. Bolingbroke's father, John of Gaunt, is one of the king's advisers and takes part in the decision about punishing Bolingbroke. John of Gaunt goes along with a penalty of temporary exile for his son. Afterwards, he tells the king that he did so solely to avoid any imputation of partiality.

Similarly, in *Measure for Measure*, Angelo is the acting magistrate while the Duke of Vienna pretends to be out of town. Isabella asks

Angelo to pardon her brother, who is under a death sentence for sleeping with his fiancée. Angelo agrees to grant the pardon but only if Isabella will sleep with him. Angelo's effort to make justice turn on such a couch payment epitomizes the corrupt judge.

So, too, does Portia's masquerade as a judge in *The Merchant of Venice*. The standard view of Portia is that she does a wonderful job of tempering law with mercy in judging the lawsuit over Shylock's loan to Antonio. Even so, she had no business in the role of judge. As William Hazlitt, the great nineteenth century English critic said, "Portia is not a very great favorite with us." She is interested in the outcome: her fiancé, Antonio's best friend, was the person for whom the loan was made. Portia's undisclosed bias stripped the blindfold from justice and tainted the judgment.

After Portia renders her tainted judgment, her fiancé, not knowing whom she is, tries to bribe her. He sends a servant to give gold to Portia. To her credit, Portia rejects the money. But at that point, of course, a bribe was superfluous. Portia's payment came in other ways. The fix was in from the start.

The descriptions of corrupt judges in Shakespeare say something about the legal ethics of the time. Then, as now, due process of law required judges to be fair and impartial. Then, as now, a biased judge violated basic rights. A judge who had a financial interest in the outcome or was related to the parties was and is rightly deemed incapable of disinterested judgment.

Doubtless Shakespeare was aware of a notable incident involving Sir Thomas More in 1533. When More, Lord Chancellor of England for a time under Henry VIII, fell out of favor with his monarch, the first charges brought against him alleged that he took bribes during his term of office. To accuse a judge of taking bribes is a serious business, one calculated to destroy a judicial reputation. If such charges could be proved, More's name among his people would have been blackened. The king's council called More before it to answer the trumped-up charges, and More acquitted himself handily. (In this respect, Robert Boalt's play *A Man for All Seasons* is historically inaccurate: More was beheaded not because he was convicted of bribe-taking, but because he opposed Henry's religious reforms.)

More's classic attitude toward bribes shows itself in his famous refusal to accept gifts. A gentleman who had a suit pending in Chancery sent his servant to More with a present of two handsome silver flagons.

More, unwilling to accept the gift, skillfully turned it aside. The gentleman, he asked, desired to taste the Chancellor's wine? "Go to my cellar," said More. "Fill thy master's ewer with my best wine. Take it home, and let thy master know I do not judge it."

A later Lord Chancellor, Sir Francis Bacon, had less luck in defending himself against bribery charges. Bacon, of course, was Shakespeare's contemporary and is even thought by some to have been the true author of Shakespeare's plays. If so, the portrayals of corrupt judges came from Bacon's first-hand knowledge of judicial bribe-taking.

In 1621, Bacon — a philosopher, writer, scientist — was Lord Chancellor and at the pinnacle of his public career. But in that year his life fell apart. Parliament drew up twenty-eight articles of impeachment against Bacon for corruption and bribery. There is no doubt Bacon accepted money from litigants (though he sometimes decided against them). At first, Bacon defended himself on the ground of custom, *i.e.*, that everybody did it. But as more and more proof surfaced, Bacon avoided a trial by resigning and confessing.

Bacon's confession, delivered as a scroll under seal to the House of Lords, was read aloud: "To the Right Honourable the Lords Spiritual and Temporal, in the High Court of Parliament assembled: The Confession and humble Submission of me, the Lord Chancellor. Upon advised consideration of the charge, descending into my own conscience, and calling my memory to account so far as I am able, I do plainly and ingenuously confess that I am guilty of corruption; and do renounce all defence, and put myself upon the grace and mercy of your Lordships. The particulars I confess and declare to be as followeth. . . ." Bacon then appended the twenty-eight charges.

Francis Bacon's bribe scandal broke five years after Shakespeare's death, so Shakespeare could not have known about it. But the first edition of Bacon's famous *Essays* came out in 1597, and was reissued in 1612, while Shakespeare was very much at work writing plays. Bacon's essays, short discourses on various topics written in the familiar clean style of the King James Bible, are a pleasure to read even today. As essayists go, Bacon ranks with Montaigne, Addison and Steele, and Macaulay as a master of the art. One of Bacon's essays is, as we lawyers like to say, right on point.

In his essay "Of Judicature," Bacon wrote: "The place of Justice is a hallowed place; And therefore, not only the Bench, but the Footpace, and Precincts, and Purpose thereof, ought to be preserved without

Scandal and Corruption . . . above all things, integrity is their [*i.e.,* judges'] portion and proper virtue."

As this eloquent passage shows, Bacon certainly understood the ground rules and the highest aspirations of justice. His many achievements in fields besides law — his important work in philosophy and natural science — only underscore the magnitude of the distance he fell. In several ways, though, Bacon in his essay "Of Judicature" was only articulating what everyone understood. Lord Edward Coke, who sat on a committee of Parliament investigating the charges against Bacon, put it tersely: "A corrupt judge is the grievance of grievances."

This was the setting in which the first folio of Shakespeare's works was published in 1623. Barely two years had passed since Bacon's disgrace. In another two years, a further revised edition of Bacon's *Essays* — including the ironic "Of Judicature" — would be off the presses. And the story of Thomas More's attitude toward bribes was part of the common heritage. Against such a background, Shakespeare's crooked judges must have been readily seen for what they in fact were.

Though much has changed since Shakespeare's day, much abides. One of the values that abides is the abhorrence of the corrupt judge. In all times, in all places, the crooked judge is anathema.

CHAPTER 7

———

A Legal Comedy
(The Comedy of Errors)

From the serious subject of crooked judges in Shakespeare's plays we move to one of his lightest pieces of fluff. But we have to be careful. For, if *The Comedy of Errors* is not one of Shakespeare's deepest works, we should still approach it knowing that laughter is often the most acceptable way of making a serious point. Jay Leno, David Letterman, and Conan O'Brien, not to mention John Stewart and Steven Colbert, are only the most recent in a long list of people who have surely taught us that much. Behind the laughter in *The Comedy of Errors* lurk several serious points, and many of them are points about law.

That *The Comedy of Errors* says something about law should come as no surprise in light of the purpose and audience of Shakespeare's plays. Some scholars have suggested that the play, certainly Shakespeare's shortest and probably his earliest, was an entertainment commissioned for a fee for a specific occasion, in this case a lawyers' celebration. It was first performed in Gray's Inn, one of the Inns of Court in London, on a feast night in 1594. From all accounts of the gala performance, the crowds of lawyers in the audience were boisterous and enjoyed themselves immensely.

The good time had by the lawyers is reflected in the play. The play seems to sum up the story again and again. One possible reason for such repetition is that the lawyers — either because they had short attention spans, were laughing too much to concentrate, or as a result of drink kept passing out during the play — needed the plot explained to them several times. Based on this incident, one can speculate why lawyers generally tend to repeat themselves so much.

To grab his legal audience at the start, Shakespeare opens the play with a legal scene. The Duke of Ephesus sentences Egeon, a merchant from Syracusa, for violating an early anti-immigration law: the Ephesian law banning all Syracusans. The law is clear and the draconian penalty no less so: death and forfeiture of goods unless the Syracusan can pay a heavy fine. Inasmuch as Egeon lacks the funds, the Duke tells him: "Therefore by law thou art condemned to die."

This opening scene already raises persistent legal issues. One such issue is capital punishment. Shakespeare does not explore the question in *The Comedy of Errors* except to raise it in all its starkness. Unlike *Measure for Measure*, Shakespeare in *The Comedy of Errors* does not have the condemned man brood aloud about the psychological horrors of being on death row. Yet, even without such explicit brooding, the severity of the punishment, applied in a discriminatory way to an outsider, touches our modern sensibilities at an exposed and raw spot.

Another legal issue raised is reliance on discriminatory laws against foreigners. Like the Alien Statute in *The Merchant of Venice*, the anti-immigration law in *The Comedy of Errors* has what to our minds would be all sorts of constitutional problems. Why does it single out all Syracusans? Why is there no individual decision-making? Where is due process?

The Duke's attitude in the first scene also relates to the rule of law. He tells the merchant to "plead no more." "I am not partial (*i.e.*, predisposed)," declares the Duke, "to infringe our laws." Is this not one way of saying, as the Founding Fathers said, that we are a government of laws and not of men? No man is above the law, not even a chief executive such as the Duke. If only our own elected officials could always say as much as the Duke did.

As so often happens in Shakespeare, a reference to the rule of law becomes a device for considering different concepts of law. On the one hand, law can be harsh and rigorous, applied to the letter. This concept is embodied in the Duke's comment, "For we may pity, though not pardon thee." It is the same idea expressed by the hypocrite Angelo in *Measure for Measure* when he refuses to bend the harsh law in that play requiring the death penalty for pre-marital sex.

On the other hand, the rigor of the law, as Portia eloquently said in *The Merchant of Venice*, should be tempered with equity and mercy. This same theme occurs in *Measure for Measure*. The Duke in *The Comedy of Errors* seems to understand this equitable concept, but only up to a point. He says:

> Now trust me, were it not against our laws,
> Against, my crown, my oath, my dignity,
> Which princes, would they, may not disannul,
> My soul should sue as advocate for thee,
> But though thou art adjudged to the death,
> And passed sentence may not be recalled
> But to our honor's great disparagement,
> Yet will I favor thee in what I can.

We see here a discussion of legal philosophy.

Some flavor of the difference between the two legal concepts comes through in contrasting pleas by litigants in the play. Later, one Angelo sounds like Shylock when he says: "Sir, sir, I shall have the law in Ephesus." Another character, Antipholus of Ephesus (one of the twins), seeks something else: "Justice, most gracious Duke! O, grant me justice . . . now grant me justice." One seeks "law" in all its rigor; the other wants "justice", which suggests a concept of law informed by equity.

The distinction drawn by Shakespeare between "law" and "justice" is familiar. The Romans distinguished between "lex" and "jus." Since then, most societies have perceived a difference between "positive law" and a "higher" or "natural law" that embodies a heavier dose of "rightness." In essence, it is the difference between "what the law is" and "what the law ought to be" as applied to specific circumstances.

Even the basic farce theme in the play has meaning for lawyers. Characters in the play get confused and make mistakes because of the two sets of twins. Characters swear they see things that in fact did not happen; hence the title *The Comedy of Errors*. But errors in perspective are what trial lawyers deal in all the time; such errors are the stuff of cross-examination and sometimes lead not to comedy but to tragedy in the legal process. The next time we sum up to a jury in the case of questionable eye-witness testimony, we can quote Shakespeare's line from this play: "What error drives our eyes and ears amiss?"

Lawyers have, since the beginning of time, played a role in collecting debts for clients. Shakespeare knew this and included some debt collection legal scenes in the play that had its debut at the Inns of Court. At one point, two different creditors say to two different debtors: "make present satisfaction,/or I'll attach you by the officer." The lawyers in the audience doubtless caught the reference to one of their main lines of work.

One of the debtors gives a modern legal response. After being arrested for nonpayment, he warns the creditor (a goldsmith): "You shall buy this sport as dear/As all the metal in your shop." Here we see the familiar legal counterattack. The debtor who thinks himself so wrongly treated will surely rely on the Elizabethan equivalent of counterclaims for malicious prosecution, abuse of process, false arrest, and motions for sanctions for proceeding in bad faith.

Beyond these specific legal references, *The Comedy of Errors* has a larger theme about law. The play is part of a Western theatrical tradition — comedy — that in some sense deals with the two basic concepts of law and equity. *The Comedy of Errors* shows that the values of resourcefulness and flexibility stand out against the codes and jargons of legalism. In the long run, as the play illustrates with its happy outcome, substance prevails over form, and the spirit mitigates the letter of the law.

Harvard literature professor Harry Levin discusses some of this in his book *Playboys and Killjoys*. Levin writes that comedy is a way of opposing repressive authority, sterile formalism, and legalism. It symbolizes the waywardness of life as against categorical rigidity. In comedy, as in Shakespeare's play, life always wins. In the practice of law, it may not always work out that way.

The comedies are only a part of Shakespeare's works. They are delightful and funny and often contain buried within them serious insights into life and human nature. But many people prefer Shakespeare's histories and tragedies because they deal on their face with more serious and substantial issues. One such issue is war.

CHAPTER 8

Shakespeare and the Law of War
(Henry V)

Several of Shakespeare's plays are filled with wars and war's violence. From the Trojan War in *Troilus and Cressida* to the War of the Roses in *Richard II*, *Henry IV*, *Henry VI*, and *Richard III*, from ancient Roman battles in *Julius Caesar* and *Antony and Cleopatra*, to the Battle of Agincourt in the Hundred Years War in *Henry V*, from the gruesome *Titus Andronicus* to the bloody *Macbeth*, war is a common and useful dramatic backdrop for Shakespeare. His frequent reliance on war should come as no surprise, for war's extreme circumstances cause great stress, and stress brings out the best and the worst in human beings, which provides wonderful material for a dramatist.

Actually, war is often a subject of literature. Almost inseparable, war and literature have been linked from the beginning of time. Think of the Bible, think of the *Iliad*. War stories — tales of glory, manhood and sacrifice — fascinate because war fascinates. People are somehow attracted to war, despite its awfulness. War is terrible, yet we love it. The stirring "band of brothers" speech Shakespeare puts in Henry V's mouth on the eve of the Battle of Agincourt seduces us with its siren song of the martial virtues and masculinity.

> He that outlives this day, and comes safe home
> Will stand a-tiptoe when this day is named,
> And rouse him at the name of Crispian
> He that shall see this day, and live old age,
> Will yearly on the vigil feast his neighbors

And say, "Tomorrow is Saint Crispian."
Then will he strip his sleeve and show his scars,
And say "These wounds I had on Crispin's day."
Old men forget; yet all shall be forgot.
But he'll remember, with advantages,
What feats he did that day.

* * *

This story shall the good man teach his son;
And Crispin Crispian shall ne'er go by,
From this day to the ending of the world,
But we in it shall be remembered —

* * *

And gentlemen in England, now abed,
Shall think themselves accursed they were not here;
And hold their manhoods cheap whiles any speaks
That fought with us upon Saint Crispin's day.

We read it or hear it — the bugles sound in our mind's ear — and we are almost ready to enlist and march off to the front. As Hemingway once told F. Scott Fitzgerald, "War is the best subject of all." Thus, we would expect Shakespeare often to use war as a setting. It would be odd for him not to.

With war playing so prominent a role, Shakespeare is even highly relevant to the law of war, and, as the United States stays embroiled in fighting wars in different places, even more so. This phenomenon of Shakespeare and the law of war merits our attention. It has caught the discerning and knowing eye of Theodor Meron, a respected judge of the International Criminal Tribunals for Rwanda and the former Yugoslavia, who has written two books on Shakespeare and the law of war. The first was *Henry's Wars and Shakespeare's Laws*, which came out in 1993 and received well-deserved critical acclaim. In that book, Meron analyzed in particular Henry's mistreatment and massacre of French prisoners of war after the Battle of Agincourt. "[W]e'll cut the throats of those we have," snarls Henry of the French POWs, "And not a man of them that we shall take/shall taste our mercy."

Meron's second book was the 1999 volume *Bloody Constraint: War and Chivalry in Shakespeare*, which is, in Meron's words, a "broader sequel" to the first book. It "expand[s] the focus from the laws of war in the strict sense to the broader system of chivalry in Shakespeare." *Bloody Constraint* is "an exploration of the chivalric values and foundations that sustained and reshaped the customs of war in the Middle Ages and the Renaissance, values that continue to surface in the legal, moral and utilitarian arguments configuring the laws and practices of war today."

Chivalry, according to Meron, means, perhaps more than anything else, the "duty to act honorably." It applies in war but also "implies an all-important code of behavior for the honorable person in civil society." Chivalry's ideals include honor, loyalty, courage, mercy, commitment to the community, and the avoidance of shame and dishonor. And Shakespeare, claims Meron, championed chivalry in his plays about war.

One of Meron's most important, intriguing, and controversial points is that the legacy of chivalry he sees in Shakespeare has "shaped our contemporary law." This point — chivalry's supposedly "enduring influence" on *our* law — is worth exploring a little. Its relevance to and lasting effect on the law of war, on which Meron focuses, are debatable. On one hand, some notions of chivalry seem to be embodied in the Geneva Conventions and other international understandings. On the other hand, in actual practice chivalry does not always seem to be the guiding light for conducting modern American wars.

The law of war has interested me ever since I was drafted into the Army in 1969, after my first year of law school, during the Vietnam War. (The government had eliminated graduate school deferments in 1968.) Following basic training, I was not sent overseas, but was instead assigned as a legal clerk in the JAG office of the First Armored Division at Fort Hood, Texas. I did not know until much later that the same day I was drafted — October 27, 1969 — the Army had preferred court-martial charges against Staff Sergeant David Mitchell, one of Lt. William Calley's platoon sergeants at the hapless Vietnamese hamlet of My Lai 4 on March 16, 1968. Not knowing of those court-martial charges that day, I could not then appreciate how they would synchronize with and affect my Army tour of duty. As it turned out, for much of 1970, my duties included helping the JAG lawyers prosecuting Mitchell's court-martial for his role in what became known as the My

Lai Massacre. (He was acquitted by a military jury composed entirely of Vietnam veterans.)

In the unfortunate and embarrassing My Lai incident, American troops led by Calley rounded up unarmed villagers — old men, women, and children — herded them into a ditch and opened fire, killing at least 175. The villagers had offered no resistance and had fired no shots at the Americans. The killing stopped only when an American helicopter pilot threatened to shoot the out-of-control Americans if they continued. That day, chivalry (except for the chopper pilot's) took a holiday.

As part of my Army work on the My Lai case, I read everything I could find in the Fort Hood libraries on the subject of war crimes. I studied the Nuremberg Trials that took place after World War II and found myself hypnotized by the powerful opening and closing statements of Justice Robert Jackson, who, at President Truman's request, took a leave of absence from the Supreme Court in order to lead the war crimes prosecution of the highest ranking Nazis. I read the controversial book by Columbia law professor and former brigadier general Telford Taylor, one of Jackson's assistants at Nuremberg, comparing Nuremberg to Vietnam. I pored over the Peers Commission Report, the official U.S. Army investigation into My Lai. I wanted to understand at least the basic principles of the law of war and why soldiers sometimes go beserk.

In 1970 I had no idea my Army crash course on the law of war would help me understand other events in other wars decades later. But they did. Even if our country's overall motivations in those more recent wars were chivalrous (or, for that matter, wise or prudent) — which is arguable — at least some of our actions since September 11 and in the wars in Iraq and Afghanistan were not marked by much chivalry.

Unchivalrous is the mildest word to describe American soldiers' gross mistreatment of Iraqi prisoners at Abu Ghraib. Unchivalrous is a charitable label for "extraordinary rendition," whereby the United States captured people in foreign countries and sent them to other countries known for using torture. Unchivalrous is too generous a term for disregard of the Geneva Conventions; establishment of military commissions without basic due process; warrantless domestic searches; and indefinite detention of Guantanamo prisoners without charge, trial, or the right of habeas corpus. Unchivalrous is a polite way to characterize America's encouragement or tolerance of torture, *i.e.*, enhanced interrogation techniques. Unchivalrous is hardly strong enough to label the occasional but intentional killing of dozens of unarmed, innocent civilians (men, women, and children) at Haditha, Iraq; the gang rape, murder and burning of a fourteen-year-old girl near al-Mahmudiah, Iraq; and executions of Iraqis in a Baghdad canal and three men in the Sunni Triangle in Iraq.

How does one even begin to explain such gross misbehavior by soldiers and government officials? My own very tentative and unscientific answer, drawn from my experience working on the My Lai case and studying war crimes — as well as from reading Shakespeare — has several components.

Overriding everything else is the reality and nature of war. War brings out the primal, it makes people violent and angry, and when the blood is up, people do cruel things they would never do otherwise. We all know from our own lives that when we lose our temper or even just our self-control, we say and do things we regret later. War magnifies that loss of control many fold. A Shakespearean case in point is Henry's mistreatment of the French prisoners at Agincourt. This psychological impact of war was well captured by five-star General George C. Marshall, who, as America's chief military strategist in World War II, knew a lot about the subject. "Once an army is involved in war," Marshall said, "there is a beast in every fighting man which begins tugging at its chains." Military training is designed in large part to take ordinary, peaceful, law-abiding citizens and to release that beast, to let the beast out of the bag.

Shakespeare tells us this explicitly and in so many words. Immediately after declaring "Once more unto the breach, dear friends, once more," Henry V pumps up his troops:

> In peace there's nothing so becomes a man
> As modest stillness and humility;
> But when the blast of war blows in our ears,
> Then imitate the action of the tiger:
> Stiffen the sinews, conjure up the blood,
> Disguise fair nature with hard-favored rage;
> Then lend the eye a terrible aspect.

Henry as military commander wants and needs the beast (the tiger) in each soldier to emerge. This transformation from Dr. Jekyll to Mr. Hyde, from David Banner to the Incredible Hulk, may help in battle, but beasts are not usually known for chivalry and can often cause collateral damage.

Embedded in the very nature of war is a volatile combination of dangerous psychological factors that contribute to cruelty. Soldiers feel a desire for revenge, and may take it out on whomever they find. They may be fatigued from fear, lack of sleep, and the stress of multiple deployments in combat zones. They may also suffer from frustration because the enemy is hard to find or inflicts death and injuries by booby traps or improvised explosive devices. These psychological elements play an important part in war cruelty.

Then there is the kind of person who becomes a soldier these days. Without a draft, we rely on a military made up solely of volunteers, and those volunteers are not representative of the society. They tend, for the most part, and especially in the enlisted ranks, not to be from the educated or privileged classes of society. While we may pay lip service to their patriotism, bravery, and self-sacrifice, the uncomfortable truth is that most people who enlist in their own national armies are no more and no less than mercenaries. Few join to serve the flag or their nation's honor. For the most part, they do so because they cannot find any better way to make a living, and find the rigors of service life less onerous than coping with the daily choices and decisions demanded of a civilian. The wars of all nations with volunteer armies are fought mainly by the underclass.

Calm consideration of all these factors makes one doubt the usual explanations for war crimes. Such cruelty is often blamed, especially by defenders of the military, on sociopaths or deviants, as aberrations perpetrated by a derelict few. This defense is understandable as it protects the institutions involved. But a more comprehensive explanation may be more accurate as well as more frightening. That explanation may turn on the nature of cruelty and the erosion of empathy. There are situations in which an individual who is not otherwise lacking in empathy may behave cruelly. In most of us empathy may be suspended temporarily, under certain circumstances. Those circumstances multiply and intensify in war, which may, more than anything else, explain why chivalry in war is uncommon.

Chivalry recently returned to some extent via the U.S. Supreme Court. War tends to breed novel legal issues that have to be resolved, and by now some of the most controversial legal issues in the wake of 9/11 have reached all the way up to the top of the judicial hierarchy, with good results for those concerned about chivalry in war time. Between 2004 and 2008, the High Court decided a quartet of important cases interpreting the law of war. Those decisions were infused with at least a dose of chivalry, even if that word was not used explicitly.

In *Rasul v. Bush*, the Court ruled in 2004 that federal civilian courts have jurisdiction to issue writs of habeas corpus to consider challenge to the legality of the detention of foreign nationals captured abroad during the War on Terror and imprisoned at Guantanamo. In the same year, the Court in *Handi v. Rumsfeld* determined that detaining individuals captured while fighting against the United States in Afghanistan for the duration of that conflict was a fundamental and accepted incident to war, but that due process required that an American citizen being held as an enemy combatant be given a meaningful opportunity to contest the factual basis for his detention before a neutral decision maker. In *Hamidan v. Rumsfeld*, the Court in 2006 held that military commissions then in place to try prisoners in the War on Terror were not authorized either by Congress or by the law of war, and that their procedures violated both the Uniform Code of Military Justice and the Geneva Conventions. Then, in 2008, the Supreme Court decided *Boumediene v. Bush*, which found that a new congressional law establishing military commissions was unconstitutional insofar as it suspended the habeas corpus rights of prisoners at Guantanamo.

Those four cases would have drawn interesting comments from Shakespeare. Running through this cluster of cases and animating them is an attempt to interpret the law of war with an element of chivalry. Chivalry is the unarticulated major premise, the silent but fundamental rationale, of those decisions.

Chivalry and the law of war lead Professor Meron to show how even today an American soldier can be court-martialed for not being chivalrous. "The mores of the knight errant eventually developed into the code of the officer and a gentleman," violation of which is still a court-martial offense. To underscore his point, Meron correctly notes that the U.S. Supreme Court in the 1974 case of *Parker v. Levy* held that "conduct unbecoming an officer and a gentleman" is neither unconstitutionally vague nor overbroad as a court-martial offense, and that the military is supposedly governed by a separate, higher standard than civilian life. Meron approves of *Parker v. Levy*.

But Meron does not say enough about *Parker v. Levy,* and his approval of that ruling is open to serious question. That five-to-three decision gave military commanders practically unbridled discretion to court-martial any officer (or any enlisted man) for almost anything. The case also upheld the prohibition against "conduct prejudicial to good order and discipline" and "conduct of a nature to bring discredit upon the armed forces." Sustaining these extraordinarily vague General Articles of military law, *Parker v. Levy* was terribly wrong when it was decided, and the passage of thirty-seven years has not made it any better.

The issues in *Parker v. Levy* also drew my attention as I worked on the My Lai court-martial. The charges against Sergeant Mitchell in that My Lai case were that his alleged conduct (assault with intent to commit murder) violated one of the General Articles, and it was my job, as a member of the prosecution team, to write a brief opposing a motion by Mitchell's defense lawyers to dismiss that charge as unconstitutionally vague. I thought about that issue a lot and came to the conclusion — which I kept to myself — that the Army's legal position was wrong. But an advocate is not the judge; as a matter of professional ethics, an advocate should advance good faith arguments on behalf of his client even if the advocate disagrees with them. I wrote the brief I was supposed to, and we won the motion, but I still had my doubts.

After my two-year stint in the Army, and freed from the constraints of the adversary system, I returned to law school and wrote a law review note taking the opposite position, arguing that the General Articles were unconstitutionally vague and overbroad. My argument was based on the fundamental notion that a criminal law must give a potential lawbreaker fair warning. Similarly, those who enforce the statute also need clear guidelines. Finally, criminal laws must not be so vague, or sweep so broadly, that they make legal as well as illegal conduct subject to prosecution, especially when such conduct deserves protection under the First Amendment.

My law review article, entitled "Taps for the Real Catch-22," was published in 1972 while *Parker v. Levy* was wending its way through the courts. By the time *Parker v. Levy* reached the Supreme Court in 1974, I had graduated from law school, passed the bar, and was working as a first-year associate in a big New York City law firm.

To my delight, various briefs and court opinions in the case had cited my law review article along the way. I wanted very much to see the outcome, so in February 1974 I took off a day from work and went to Washington to hear the Supreme Court oral argument in the case. It was my first time at the High Court and I was duly impressed. Arguing for the government to uphold the vague military laws was one of my former law school professors, Robert Bork, who was then Solicitor General of the United States and who would later have an unpleasant and unsuccessful confirmation battle after he was nominated to the Court by Ronald Reagan in 1987.

Although the Court ultimately rejected my position, I was pleased to see that Justice Potter Stewart's dissent cited my article three times and even cribbed several sentences from it. You can imagine how thrilled I was that an essay I had written as a law student was used in a Supreme Court opinion, even if it was a dissent. Shortly after the decision came down, Justice Stewart wrote me a gracious letter, which I framed and have kept ever since on my office wall, in which he said my article had "provided more than a little inspiration" for his dissent. I really appreciated that gesture. There is nothing like a kind and generous thank you note from a Supreme Court justice to encourage and, to borrow Justice Stewart's words, "provide more than a little inspiration" to a newly minted young attorney to spend his life in the law.

Parker v. Levy eventually will be overruled, when a more enlightened Supreme Court will see through the empty rhetoric of the 1974 decision and muster a majority to hold that American citizens do not lose their constitutional rights when they become soldiers, except to the extent absolutely necessary. It is ironic, even hypocritical, that we deny some of the most basic constitutional rights to those whose patriotism, self-sacrifice, and valor we say we admire so much.

Parker v. Levy also illuminates Professor Meron's comments about just and unjust wars. According to Meron, chivalry impelled a medieval prince to try hard to demonstrate that military action taken in his name was "just." He quotes one authority who said: "[i]f a subject is convinced of the injustice of a war, he aught not to serve in it, even in the command of his prince."

But no government ever admits its war is "unjust." That is the problem. Dr. Howard Levy — the Army captain charged in *Parker v. Levy* — like many others, was convinced of the injustice of the Vietnam War, but was court-martialled for that opposition. And what about the law of conscientious objection? Serious clashes occur here. American constitutional law does not allow an individual to select which wars he will take part in.

Let us take Meron another step further. Substitute "litigation" for "war" and see what happens. Let us apply the concept of chivalry to lawyers and call it civility. Civility among lawyers has been a hot topic for the last few decades. In the 1990s, the Chief Judge of New York promulgated a code of civility for lawyers. And the Code of Professional Responsibility proscribes "conduct that is prejudicial to the administration of justice" or "that adversely reflects on [a lawyer's] fitness to practice law."

Similarly, the U.S. House of Representatives ethics rules state that the members should conduct themselves "at all times in a manner that shall reflect creditably on the House." This provision was mentioned in connection with the 2011 scandal surrounding Congressman Anthony Weiner's inappropriate use of social media.

But can such imprecise standards — such aspirational goals — ever be thus codified? Should they? As Meron points out, chivalry is customary not statutory. "Seldom if ever realized in full, those ideals remained a source of inspiration." They apparently fulfill a lasting human need.

Shakespeare, says Meron, seems to support "a society in which law should be respected and leaders held to higher standards of civilized behavior." That is what the majority in *Parker v. Levy* said about the military.

"We need to invigorate," concludes Meron, "chivalry's concept and culture of values, especially the notion of individual honor and dishonor as motivating factors for the conduct of both warriors and citizens." And lawyers, perhaps. Here is one more link between Shakespeare and the law, a link that carries special weight and poignancy in this difficult time in our nation's history.

Another link focuses on the supposedly dishonorable conduct of one of England's least popular kings.

CHAPTER 9

More on Richard III

Who wrote Shakespeare? is not the only old open question about the Bard and his plays. Another such question concerns Richard III and the mystery of the princes in the Tower. It is a murder mystery, and to try to solve that mystery we might usefully look to the law.

By now law has taken on a well-known, increasingly useful, and distinctly interdisciplinary coloring. "Law and economics" is perhaps only the most prominent and successful such interdisciplinary approach. "Law and literature" is another. But these are only examples. Law is primarily a way of thinking, a method of analysis for studying many kinds of problems, non-legal as well as legal.

Certain historical events also readily yield to legal analysis. Did Socrates get a fair trial from his fellow Athenians? Ask some lawyers. Was Pilate's trial of Jesus appropriate? Check with lawyers. Were the trials that led to the beheadings of King Charles I and King Louis XVI in the English and French Revolutions justifiable? See a lawyer.

Very much in this tradition is the controversial case of England's last Plantagenet king, Richard III (1452-1485). Shakespeare famously portrayed him as a murderous monster and heartless usurper. According to Shakespeare, Richard, brother to King Edward IV, kills his other brother, his own wife, the deposed King Henry VI, and Henry's son Edward Lancaster (the Prince of Wales), as well as King Edward's own sons and young heirs (Richard's nephews) — the luckless princes in the Tower. And Shakespeare being Shakespeare, his dramatic hatchet job on Richard has indelibly etched our negative image of Richard and permeated the public mind ever since the early 1600s.

Shakespeare's one-sided version has not gone unchallenged. Over the centuries Richard III has gathered to his banner a number of reputable and articulate defenders. A rich, extensive and often polemical literature — mostly written by historians but not only — has grown up around Richard III's reputation, focusing in particular on the murder of the princes in the Tower. One of the most popular such books was and still is a 1951 detective novel by Josephine Tey called *The Daughter of Time*, in which a convalescing Scotland Yard inspector studies the case and concludes that Richard is innocent.

But what, we might reasonably ask, is the truth about Richard III and the princes? Perhaps we should consult a lawyer.

That is where the 1998 book *Royal Blood: Richard III and the Mystery of the Princes* by Bertram Fields comes in. The author is a lawyer, but no ordinary lawyer. Bert Fields is a prominent and highly successful entertainment trial lawyer in Los Angeles, as well as the author of two novels. He brings to bear all his ample legal and literary skills in analyzing the evidence for and against Richard to answer the question: "Were the two young princes murdered by Richard in the Tower of London?" The result is a fine addition to the growing literature on this vexing subject, what Fields calls "history's greatest unsolved mystery."

Fields starts his quest with vaulting hopes and great ambition. The "aim" of his book, he tells us, is "to explore and evaluate the arguments on each side, to weigh the evidence and, peering through the mist of centuries, to come as close as possible to the elusive truth." But, as often happens, the particular result reached in trying to solve a difficult problem is less important than the intellectual exercise in getting there. Finding the "elusive truth" may not matter as much as the process.

Accomplished and experienced litigator that he is, Fields goes about a careful, lawyerly, but non-academic consideration (without footnotes) of the most important factors: motive, opportunity, means and proclivity, together with physical evidence and other relevant facts. This quest is the heart of the book, a painstaking review and lucid analysis, and is Fields's most significant contribution. Fields recognizes the difficulties facing him, that "the most important facts are not *known*" and that many of the sources of information are highly suspect and biased, if not completely unreliable.

Despite Fields's best efforts, however, by the end of his new book the "elusive truth" still remains elusive; "history's greatest unsolved mystery" still remains unsolved. Predicting the outcome of a criminal case against Richard is, says Fields, "relatively easy." Richard, writes Fields with self-assurance, "would be acquitted of the crime by virtually any jury that heard the case." The possibility that no murders took place, that they were committed by someone else, together with the lack of admissible evidence against Richard, easily leads, thinks Fields, to reasonable doubt.

Going beyond the confines of a criminal trial, Fields asks "whether Richard's guilt is or is not probable" and what is the "degree of its probability." But even here Fields arrives at an agnostic conclusion. "An objective analysis of the facts known today," he says at the end, "does not allow for certainty or even near certainty as to Richard's innocence or guilt." He accepts the possibility of more certainty if DNA tests on bones found in the Tower in 1674 prove helpful. But for now, for Fields, "the soundest conclusion" resembles that of many philosophers who have tried to prove the existence of God: that "we do not know the answer, that the mystery remains unsolved." Shades of the Shakespeare authorship debate!

Fields's book omits one highly relevant line of inquiry. A reader might expect Fields, the fabled Hollywood lawyer, to comment on Shakespeare's *Richard III* as a problem of libel in fiction or docudrama. If, as many believe, Shakespeare badly maligned Richard III, the natural question for an entertainment lawyer becomes how much leeway does an author, playwright or screenwriter have with historical facts?

Fields does not ask this question. As a result, he does not tell us whether he would hold Shakespeare liable for defamation under such circumstances. It would have been interesting to learn Fields's views on the thorny and as yet unresolved issue of libel in fiction. For that is at least one of the broad and contemporary legal issues stirred by Richard's historical guilt or innocence.

As to this issue and Richard's responsibility for the disappearance of the princes, Fields may have the best last word. "Perhaps we will never know," Fields says. Probing deeper, he adds: "Perhaps that's what makes the subject so interesting."

Thus we arrive at the same conclusion in this context as we did with the debate over who wrote Shakespeare.

CHAPTER 10

Shakespeare Finds an Agent
(Or an Agent's Midafternoon Dream)

My one-person literary agency was doing poorly. After Raymond Chandler died, I gave up private-eye work and moved to the Big Apple to see if I could make it in the literary game as an agent. I had visions of how I was going to rep only the best authors, a winning combo of the most literary and the most lucrative writers. But things hadn't exactly worked out that way.

I hadn't reeled in a new author in months, much less sold a manuscript. My royalty commissions had dwindled to a trickle. My unpaid bills were mounting, and two weeks ago I had to let my secretary go. With nothing to do but wait for the phone to ring, I started to drink and smoke and eat red meat again, and, worst of all, spend endless hours staring blankly out the dirty window of my small, sparsely furnished office, feeling sorry for myself.

In this dreamlike state of depression, I surprised myself by muttering something I had memorized fifty years ago in high school. "When in disgrace with fortune and men's eyes," I recited, "I all alone beweep my outcast state." My eyes misted as I recalled that sonnet and how precisely it captured my current feelings.

Then the phone rang, its harsh jangle snapping me out of my self-pity. I picked up the receiver and gave my stock answer: "Immortal Literary Agency, Marlowe speaking." The voice on the other end had a vague English accent.

"Is this Philip Marlowe?"

"Yes, who's this?"

"*The* Philip Marlowe who used to be a detective on the west coast and whose ancestor was Christopher Marlowe, the Elizabethan writer?"

"Yes. What business is it of yours? Who is this?"

"Good. This is Bill Shakespeare, and have I got a job for you!"

Uh oh, I thought to myself, another New York full-mooner. What did I do to deserve this? But all I could spit out was, "Who the hell are you? And what are you talking about?"

"Listen, Marlowe, you're a literary agent, right?"

"Yeah."

"Literature is your family heritage, right?"

"Yeah."

"And I'm an author, right?"

"A dead one. In fact, the worst kind: a dead white European male. You're the big enchilada."

"I can't believe you said that, you who a minute ago were quoting one of my poems. Don't you remember what I wrote? 'So long as men can breathe, or eyes can see,/So long lives this.' Or, 'Not marble, not the gilded monuments/ Of princes, shall outlive this powerful rhyme.' And, 'Death to me subscribes, / Since, spite of him, I'll live in this poor rhyme.' I am immortal, I decided 'to be' rather than 'not to be,' and you are the proprietor of the Immortal Literary Agency. You've read about time travel, I assume?"

"Yeah."

"You know H.G. Wells' famous story? You know about Woody Allen's 'Kugelmass Episode'? And you surely have read Jack Finney's *Time and Again*, right?"

"Of course. Even though I didn't handle any of those authors, I know their work and their time machine stuff, but that's science fiction."

"Not at all. Here I am, just like Doctor Who. Your recitation of the first two lines of my sonnet unlocked the door of the time machine. Now let's get down to business."

My head was spinning, but the fellow on the phone talked so fast, he had to be a writer, a lawyer, a politician, or a salesman. I couldn't get a word in edgewise. And, besides, my luck had about run out, so I figured what the hell, what was there to lose from hearing the guy's spiel?

"Marlowe, here's the deal. I need an agent bad. Everyone's ripping me off, been doing so for centuries. Millions of copies of my plays and poems have been sold without any royalties for me. My plays have even been made into hit Hollywood films, Broadway shows, operas and ballets, but I get nothing from them. It's an outrage.

"I thought Olivier was bad, but this Branaugh guy is too much with his movies. First it's *Henry V*, then *Much Ado About Nothing*; and *Othello* and *Hamlet*. Enough is enough! And let's not forget about Ian McKellan's *Richard III*, or that souped-up version of *Romeo and Juliet*, or Helena Bonham Carter's *Twelfth Night*. I've been biding my time ever since Olivier died. Now we —*you* — have to do something!

"And look at my stuff on Broadway. Al Pacino in *The Merchant of Venice* was a sellout. Tickets to the Royal Shakespere Company performances at the Armory cost $250 apiece. A few years ago *The Tempest* had a successful run, as did *Hamlet* and *A Midsummer Night's Dream*. What about the Public's 'Shakespeare Marathon'? *King Lear* was sold out before it opened. Sure, I get billing, but that just filches from me my good name, the immediate jewel of my soul. I don't get any money, and that makes me poor indeed. Even the Globe paid me something.

"Moving right along: I need you to look out for my interests, to get my current and back royalties up to date. I want to prevent my copyrights from being infringed. And since American copyrights now last for life plus fifty years, and I am immortal, you have a lot of work cut out for you. You've got to get on the stick about my subsidiary rights, especially this whole electronic rights stuff. I hear my collected works are now on the web. Where are my royalties? A royalty, a royalty! My kingdom for a royalty!

"You should look into getting me consulting deals on movies and plays. Check with a lawyer about suing to protect my right of publicity. You've got a lot to do, Marlowe. What are you waiting for?"

"Speaking of lawyers, Mr. Shakespeare — if that's who you really are — my attorney always tells me to reduce any agreement to writing. I'll fax over my standard agency form: two years, fifteen percent for American book and serial rights, twenty percent for film and television rights, and twenty-five percent for foreign rights. OK?"

"Who do you think you're talking to, Marlowe? This is Bill Shakespeare. Make it seven and a half percent across the board."

"Ten percent and it's a deal."

"Done. And if you do a good job, I'll introduce you to Jane Austen and Charlie Dickens. They're looking for agents now too."

"Great, but two more things before you hang up. First, do you currently have an agent? If so, you'll have to tell that agent you're switching and work out a settlement. Second, why me? There are thousands of other literary agents in New York, just about all of them with better track records than I. Why me, Philip Marlowe, ex-tec?"

"Simple, pal. My old agent died, and your family. Your ancestor Kit was a friend of mine. He got killed in a barroom brawl, when he was only twenty-nine, over whether he had secretly written my stuff. He went to his grave denying he was my ghostwriter. In return for his sacrifice, I promised myself I would help out his family. It was Marlowe, you know, and not Bacon or the others, who sometimes helped me with my writing. But that's another story."

"I think I can sell it." Visions of a million dollar advance, a paperback auction, and a movie deal danced before my eyes. "How fast can you write up a three-page proposal?"

"Tomorrow and tomorrow and tomorrow."